Fourteen of Twenty

HELLFIRE LANDING

The UK threat of mainland attack, as we stand today, remains at 'substantial'. This means that a terrorist attack remains a strong possibility and could occur without warning.

Figures revealed that the number of terror arrests had risen by sixty per cent in the year to September 2012.

Hellfire Landing is based on what could happen if real-world terrorists decide to launch a coordinated attack within the UK. A major disaster could happen at any moment, and in just five minutes could affect the lives of thousands of persons in the UK.

Could it really happen? Yes, and the consequences could be mind-blowingly catastrophic. And, yes, it could happen in any country in the world which has similar infrastructures to those in the UK.

HELLFIRE LANDING

David Hughes

ARTHUR H. STOCKWELL LTD
Torrs Park, Ilfracombe, Devon, EX34 8BA
Established 1898
www.ahstockwell.co.uk

British Library Cataloguing-in-Publication Data.
A catalogue record for this book is available
from the British Library.

This is an entirely fictional story,
and no conscious attempt has been made
to accurately record or recreate
any real-life events.

By the same author:
Purple Jade
Cloned Identity
One in a Million

ISBN 978-0-7223-4342-5
Printed in Great Britain by
Arthur H. Stockwell Ltd
Torrs Park   Ilfracombe
Devon EX34 8BA

CHAPTER ONE

This story begins in an office system located in London's Downing Street, SW1A 2AA. Downing Street is located in Whitehall in Central London, a few minutes' walk from the Houses of Parliament and a little farther from Buckingham Palace. The street was built in the 1680s by Sir George Downing (c.1623–84) on the site of a mansion called Hampden House. The houses on the west side of the street were demolished in the nineteenth century to make way for government offices, now occupied by the Foreign and Commonwealth Office.

Downing Street has for over 200 years housed the official residences of two of the most senior British cabinet ministers: the First Lord of the Treasury, an office now synonymous with that of Prime Minister of the UK, and the Second Lord of the Treasury, an office held by the Chancellor of the Exchequer. The Prime Minister's official residence is 10 Downing Street; the Chancellor's official residence is next door at Number 11. The government's Chief Whip has an official residence at Number 12, though the current chief whip's residence is at Number 9.

The office nicknamed the Cab in Downing Street is the worldwide communication hub, the listening and watching centre of the UK and the world. It monitors events in real time and analyses what happens within the government minute by minute. The office is staffed and maintained twenty-four hours a day, seven days a week, 365 days a year. The Cab has five persons working on three shifts with a weekly change-round. Three listeners have headphones and operate complex workstations, which they can access with their own logic key together with their fingerprints via a complex log-in system. A fourth person acts as a replacement to allow stand-down break times. That person, the controller, sits behind and above the listeners, who constantly monitor several screens on the wall. The controller can direct a listener's viewing to any of the screens; he is in control of the viewing patterns. The controller also looks for any problems that may arise and deals quickly with them. The fifth person sits next to the controller and has direct access through the phone and radio systems to the emergency services. He will inform the controller if a happening on any screen is being dealt with by any of the emergency services.

There are three other persons, intermediaries who control the flow of information to and from the Prime Minister's office and other government departments. They ensure that data obtained by the office is passed on to the relevant departments. They are in a separate office from the main Cab room, but they can see into the Cab office through a thick, double-glazed, large, one-way window. They also have sound communication with the controller, but this is one-way. The controller cannot hear or see any persons in the room behind him. Also the controller and the listeners have their own workrooms and toilet facilities. When entering or leaving the building, they can only go to their own designated work areas; they cannot bump into or commutate with any other person.

All the information received via television, satellite, phone, Internet and radio is constantly electronically recorded, together with automatic backup on several servers located in different departments. This information is logged and saved as read-only, and cannot be changed, saved or printed without prior clearance. The storage servers are themselves backed up automatically via multiple fireproof cable links in a vast array of fireproof rooms, called the dungeons, located deep underground in a nuclear bunker. This bunker can only be accessed using multiple access codes and secret protocol knowledge. The access method is under constantly review and personnel are frequently changed as a security measure.

The Prime Minister's principle personal secretary has access to all the offices and can visit at any time to ensure all is well. He is the one who decides whether or not to contact the Prime Minister immediately – which could mean get him out of bed in an emergency. The principle personal secretary is contacted whenever it is felt that a happening might be important. The controller has a red button he can use if necessary to alert the Prime Minister's secretary in his office. A pulsing sound and flashing light will continue until the Prime Minister's secretary flicks his cancelling switch. This will also inform the intermediaries' office that the panic alert had been received. The secretary will then quickly go to the intermediaries' office rather than spend time responding by phone.

There are three persons designated as the Prime Minister's secretary, and this is to ensure that there is always one on duty. At times, the Prime Minister's principle secretary may accompany him when he leaves Downing Street for any function. The principle secretary is in close communication with the duty secretary at Downing Street and is regularly updated and informed of any issues that might need immediate attention by the Prime Minister. The Prime Minister will immediately change his schedule if a more important issue needs his urgent attention.

In the intermediaries' office communication with the controller takes place using a speaker system. To ensure that information is not lost by lack of attention, it is automatically recorded and can be instantly repeated. This is particularly useful in an emergency when only one person or no persons are in the office when communication is received..

In the Cab office at 5 p.m. one Tuesday, data was being logged that there had been a plane crash at London's Heathrow Airport. The information was coming from the emergency services and the media, but as yet there were few details. The controller notified the intermediaries.

The intermediaries discussed the information and decided not to inform the Prime Minister's secretary. They asked the controller to ensure that the listeners were focused on relaying information as soon as it appeared. They were aware that the facts would become clearer when the media circus arrived at Heathrow with their satellite vans and started transmitting on-scene information.

At five thirty the emergency services reported difficult access to Heathrow because of traffic. There was complete gridlock, and it was requested that media helicopters be allowed airspace over the area. Soon the media circus had a helicopter in the air and film was being relayed showing a scene of total confusion. Ambulances and fire engines were trying in vain to get through. As word got round, the traffic situation became chaotic. The normal rush-hour traffic was increased by sightseers converging on the road system around Heathrow.

The media helicopter was also transmitting pictures of flames and a rising plume of waving black smoke inside the airport, but the helicopter was still too far away to show clearly what had happened.

The Prime Minister's principle secretary now entered the intermediaries' office and he said, "I was watching the television in my room. Is any further information available? I am not sure if I should yet bother the Prime Minister."

The intermediaries switched on the television receiver in their office just in time to watch as a media helicopter moved into the airspace above Heathrow.

"John, what the hell are they doing? They know they are not supposed to enter that area. That is restricted airspace for a very good reason."

"Well, I don't know, secretary. I expect they are trying to get closer to the accident scene so as to get the best possible pictures."

"That may be so, but the downdraft from the rotor blades could fan the flames and make matters even worse. Also they could get in the way of a plane trying to land or take off as well as any emergency personnel trying to get to the scene. John, contact MP [Metropolitan Police Control Centre] at Scotland Yard, and tell them to get those idiots out of that area. Tell them to arrest the paper's editor if they have to."

(All 999 phone calls made in the London area go straight to Scotland Yard, which then establishes contact with the control room of the relevant police force. The local police force then takes control using its local radio system. Written details of the incident is faxed from Scotland Yard to the local force for them to log. MP also monitors the local police radio networks, and if the situation requires assistance from other forces or special units, like CO19, the firearms response unit, they then ask the attending police patrol car to switch their in-car radio to another band so they can deal with them direct and bypass the local radio connection. They can also instruct that patrol car to abandoned the call as it is being dealt with by others. This could happen if the arrival of a police patrol would be detrimental to the situation in hand.)

"Wow! Too late, secretary! The media helicopter has now crashed. It has smashed into the ground, down in flames and with massive carnage."

"Jesus Christ! My God, John, what happened? Did you see what caused that?"

"It was so quick. It just burst into flames and fell out of the sky. It crashed into the ground and disintegrated all over the place. Another camera recorded the disaster from some way away, outside the airport perimeter, probably from on top of one of those vans the media use."

"Oh well, at least they now have got a good picture to show on the television. I mean, they missed the plane crashing (if that is what happened) and now they seem to have made a crash of their very own."

"Poor devils, secretary! I can't see anybody surviving that. I don't know how many were on board, but I am sure some families won't be having Daddy or Mummy home for tea tonight."

"You're right. It's sickening when you think. And now we have lost the only aerial coverage we had. Is there nothing more yet?"

"No, secretary. Until we get a camera inside the airport we shan't have any details of what has happened or how many casualties there are. The helicopter deaths have increased the tally – let's hope we don't have any more now."

"Well, I will go and bring the Prime Minister up to date so he is not too in the dark. Let me know if there are any more developments."

"John, what's happened? I had only just got back to my office. What's the alert? What has happened?"

"Updates have just come through from MP at Scotland Yard. They have lost contact with their unit at Heathrow. They think that plane crash is probably more serious than first thought and it has probably hit and demolished, or damaged, part of Terminal 5 and/or its satellite buildings. That's the terminal where they have a spanking-new operations room. An off-duty police constable phoned in and let them know. We thought it was serious enough to push the red button."

"You are right, John. I'd better inform the Prime Minister. It looks like the casualty list could be high. Make sure the listeners are focused on the emergency services – the ambulance and hospital services will probably give the best information."

"John, that certainly took the smile off his face. The secretary sure looked glum, to say the least."

"Probably he is working out that his yearly weekend in Scotland could now be cancelled. What does he actually do in Scotland, then? Is it something special, by any chance?"

"Special, yes, to him. He goes up this time every year and walks on the wild side. He stays at some old Scottish inns and drinks the local-made moonshine. He enjoys it so much and comes back with a big smile. Old Jock, the cook in the kitchen, told me he does the same a bit later in the year, and Jock comes from the area the secretary visits. Jock has relatives still living there; they tell him what the Prime Minister gets up to, but the secretary doesn't know about Jock or what he knows – nudge, nudge. You know, John, there seems to be something making my bones itch – this Heathrow business, I mean. If they have a crash, they are all geared up to cope with the situation. If a plane's hit a terminal, that is just a small area; you would think we would be getting information from the other terminals. It seems too quiet – very much too quiet for my liking."

"Yeah, I can see what you are saying, but give it a thought for a minute. Those planes carry a lot of fuel – some 50,000 gallons. Back in the old days the planes used to dump any fuel they had on board before they landed, but now it's different. Because of the cost they don't dump any excess. It depends if it was a short- or long-haul flight how much it landed with, but the fuel could have sprayed over a large area so you could be looking at fires everywhere. They could be spending all their time and energy trying to contain them. Then you could also have a few hundred casualties to look after as well."

"Yes, I see what you mean. We have not had a big crash area before inside the airport. Remember that one back in the seventies, when that plane, that Trident, came down after take-off just a couple of miles from the perimeter. That seemed big at the time, and the emergencies services had trouble getting there because of sightseers, but that didn't cause any problems in the airport. Also when that one came down in Southall the airport was missed. I think Lockerbie is the biggest plane crash I can remember and that made a big hole in the ground, but it only damaged a few houses. Let's hope the Heathrow one is not any bigger. It's a bit too close to home. Regarding what you were saying about the fuel dumping, many years ago a friend lived under the flight path on the Windsor side and he was always complaining about his car being covered in sticky stuff. At first he thought it was sap from the trees in the road, but then he found out it was caused by the fuel the planes were dumping."

"Blimey O'Reilly! We have a lot more verbal going on now. It seems to be coming from all directions – coming from everywhere thick and fast."

"Yeah, I forgot about them. You don't think about all those passengers stuck up in the clouds with nowhere to go. Some of them must have been going round for a while, and some of the planes could be getting low on fuel. They'll be getting desperate to land somewhere, but they can't land until the runway is clear and safe."

"I wonder how many are waiting to land. They say one lands and one takes off every minute, so sixty planes every hour, and we are – what? – three hours since the initial crash. There could be over a hundred planes now looking for somewhere to land, and more will be joining the queue every minute. Has anything been done to divert them to other airports? This is going to cause widespread chaos. There will be planes sitting on runways in foreign countries which can't take off because there is nowhere to land in the UK."

"That's right. I know we have quite a few airports scattered around, but Heathrow is the biggest; if that is totally closed, there will be more planes in the air than there are spaces on the ground. The other airports will reach capacity quickly. A lot of British persons may be dumped in Europe and have to walk or swim home. It could be like another Dunkirk. Mind you, at least we now have the Channel Tunnel. It's just as well that wasn't built back in 1945 or we could have had our army lads coming back down one tunnel and the German army with their tanks and Adolf coming down the other."

"Hi, secretary. What's new on the Heathrow crash? Any more news?"

"Well, Prime Minister, it's not looking good. We have been receiving sketchy reports. The media circus crashed a helicopter while trying to obtain closer pictures. The emergency services have found it difficult to reach the airport owing to the rush-hour traffic and sightseers who are parking up on the roads which lead to the airport – especially the M25 and M4. They're all gridlocked and accidents have been caused by the smoke from the airport. There hasn't yet been any direct communication with the airport."

"Secretary, you mention emergency services – does that mean Heathrow doesn't have the facilities to deal with a serious plane crash?"

"They can deal with most things, Prime Minister, but we think a terminal building has been hit. We don't know yet exactly how many casualties there are, but we may need to make, say, a hundred paramedics available, as well as extra ambulances and hospital beds."

"Secretary, I need to alert every hospital in the area, and I need to know if any VIPs are involved. I don't want the media to know before I do that the king and queen or premier of any nation is caught up in this. Do you follow my thinking? If not the crashed plane, they could be on one which is diverted. They might need looking after. We'll have to help them with transport, security and accommodation."

"Yes, Prime Minister. It is all in hand. I am checking every avenue as they might not be on our official list. They could be just visiting without the usual protocol, but I'll make sure they are given the same treatment regarding security, etc."

"Secretary, you have news – and it is good, I hope?"

"Prime Minister, I need to inform you of another matter that seems to need your immediate attention."

"Very well, secretary. What has happened that has caused you concern?"

"Prime Minister, the American Embassy – their operations man, Mike Sawyer, has just phoned. He wants to know if we have switched on Cobra yet."

(Cobra meetings are named after Cabinet Office Briefing Room A in Whitehall. Cobra is an emergency response committee, a get-together of ministers, civil servants, the police, intelligence officers and others appropriate to whatever emergency they are looking into. When the government announces that it has convened a Cobra meeting, it can give one of two impressions. The first is that it is quickly getting to grips with a thorny issue of immediate national significance. The other is that something bad is happening and maybe they are to blame. So those in government are very careful in their use of language. Sometimes it is useful for them to sound reassuring. Sometimes, conscious of the potential for a mass outbreak of media hype, it is more useful for them to talk down the significance of such a meeting. The build-up to the Olympics was a case in point. With just a few days to go until the opening ceremony, the Prime Minister chaired a meeting involving senior ministers, Olympic organisers and those responsible for security. Keeping the Games safe, making sure transport works as well as can be expected and dealing with the threat of strikes were the main themes up for discussion, we were told. It was described by many as a Cobra meeting – one of many that took place before and during the Olympic Games. But Downing Street sources insisted that it wasn't a Cobra meeting. Clearly if it looks like a Cobra and it sounds like a Cobra, it doesn't necessarily mean it is a Cobra.)

"Secretary, now just hold fire a minute, Why exactly does Sawyer want to know if we've switched on cobra? Does he know something we don't?"

"I have heard nothing about switching on Cobra. We have had no reason to do so. The special services and MI5 have been totally quiet lately."

"Secretary, this still bothers me. Mike Sawyer is CIA, and they always seem to be ahead of the game. They always seem to be in front of us."

"That is so, Prime Minister, but that is because the CIA usually start the game in the first place. As you know, the Americans insisted that we have one of their people in Cobra and they nominated Mike Sawyer; he wasn't our choice."

"We know that, secretary, but having an American in the group makes a lot of sense. It gives us quick access to any important information and enables us to counter terrorist activity which without the Americans we probably wouldn't know about until we are attacked."

"I see your reasoning, Prime Minister, but I sometime feel we are always giving the Americans far more than we are receiving. It's as though we are being used as a pawn in a complex situation. It worries me that we seem to be jumping around to the Americans' music all the time when we are actually out of tune."

"Anyway, secretary, I am bothered – bothered because here we now have a situation at Heathrow which, let's agree, is completely out of the normal; but, even so, we should have emergency procedures to cope. And we now have a phone call from the CIA asking us if we have switched on Cobra, which is a group of persons to advise and counter a threat to our well-being. Are the two related? We need to find out and find out quickly, secretary. I want you to notify the available Cobra persons and put them on standby. Let's be safe, not sorry."

"Right, I will arrange that straight away, Prime Minister."

"Prime Minister, this is the list of available Cobra members.

Another fact has just been revealed by our special sources: the Americans have now operated a lockdown procedure at all their bases in the UK."

"Secretary, what does 'lockdown' mean exactly? Is it just a normal procedure that doesn't, or shouldn't, bother us?"

"Prime Minister, no, it's not completely normal. They brought it in after the 9/11 attack in New York. It means they have upgraded their security to the highest level so no one can get in or out unless the top brass say so – not even the American president."

"Good grief, secretary! Do you think they are expecting some sort of mass attack? If so, from where, when, by whom and how? And how will we respond? After all, if someone is attacking the American bases in the UK, that is more than just on our doorstep; that's part of our own country being attacked."

"Well, Prime Minister, we have not been alerted about any sort of imminent attack, and I am sure we would be told if the Americans suspected there would be a strike against a base in the UK. This could be just an exercise – to test their own procedures and to see how we react. I can remember, from years gone by, how they used to have their fighter planes flying about the UK, trying to creep up on their own bases to test their readiness in case of a Russian attack. One at Upper Heyford rings a bell and one up in Norfolk somewhere, as well as a base up north."

"Secretary, I want you to start Cobra. Switch it on. Alert the available members immediately and inform Mike Sawyer, so he can attend. That way we might find out what they are up to before we end up with egg on our faces. And ask the Foreign Secretary to see me."

"Prime Minister, Mike Sawyer to see you."

"Hello, Mike. Nice to see you again."

"Prime Minister, I was pleased to see you have switched on Cobra, but I am not here just because of that. Prime Minister, you could probably have terrorist activity at Heathrow."

"Really, Mike? We have a plane crash – not routine, I know, but these things can happen and it is something we know about and are dealing with. I know nothing about terrorists causing this."

"Prime Minister, I have had the Pentagon on the line. They have stated that their satellite surveillance of Heathrow indicates that the incident was not an accident."

"Mike, so you don't actually have concrete reasons to blame terrorists?"

"No, Prime Minister. At the moment it is probably just a gut feeling. We have not been able to contact any of our airline persons at the airport, but a plane hitting a terminal is reminiscent of a movie I saw some time back. It is the sort of idea one of our terror groups might like to carry out. London might be an easier target than New York."

"Mike, I remember that film. As I recall, there wasn't much damage done to the plane or to the building."

"That's right, Prime Minister, but that was a film – just a spoof film about a plane running off the runway with no brakes and a humorous pilot and parking itself inside the terminal building. If it had been true to life, it would have been a different matter."

"Mike, I appreciate your concern, but I want to err on the side of caution. I'm not about to push the panic button. We are talking about a large populated area – millions of persons. We need to evaluate the situation from all perspectives before we take any action that could cause wholesale panic and disruption as well as umpteen casualties and then turn out to have been unnecessary."

"OK, Prime Minister, I will follow your reasoning and join Cobra members and see how we go. If necessary we can mobilise forces very quickly – both land and air."

"Secretary, I need the senior army officer in this vicinity. I would like him here now, as well as the Deputy Prime Minister and all other cabinet members."

(The Chief of the General Staff (CGS) is the professional head of the army, with responsibility for developing and generating military capability from an integrated army (regular and reserve) and for maintaining the fighting effectiveness, efficiency and morale of the service. The CGS reports to the Chief of the Defence Staff (CDS) and as a service Chief of Staff (COS) has a right of direct access to the Secretary of State and the Prime Minister. He is the principal military adviser to the Secretary of State for Defence and the government. The other services (RAF and navy) have their equivalents of the CGS, who report to the CDS as well.)

"Right, ladies and gentlemen, I have called this meeting because we have a mini crisis building up into a major crisis. I'm sure you are all aware of the possible plane crash at Heathrow. I will tell you now that the Americans seem to be treating this as a terrorist attack. The CIA are involved in some way. They seem to have more detailed information than we do at present. I am under the impression that there are American ships close by waiting to deploy their special forces all round London to take control. Their air force outnumbers ours; they have considerable firepower already stationed at bases on our soil. Has anyone any relevant information to share with us."

"Prime Minister, I know the newest American aircraft carrier, the USS *George H. W. Brush*, will be anchoring just off Portsmouth in a few days' time. It's too big to enter Portsmouth Harbour. It is on a goodwill visit and it will have other ships, including submarines, in attendance as escorts. I could not say how many marines are on board, but we could probably find out from the Admiralty. I do know it's very big – ginormous. It carries in excess of seventy aircraft from eight squadrons on a 4.5-acre flight deck, and has 3,200 sailors and 2,480 air-force personnel. I believe it is bigger than any one of our RAF bases. Oh, this information came from the Internet and not from my head. I have my department looking for any other information we can glean from other sources."

"Do that, Defence Secretary, and get all the information you can without rattling anybody's cage. We need to keep the lid on this. We have a few million persons close by and we don't want to start a wholesale panic; so it's important to release only safe information through our press department. I don't want anyone spreading insensitive, false or damaging information. There won't be any pats on the back, but more like kicks up the backside, for anyone who releases any information without my knowledge. Anybody else?"

"What about the American bases we have in the UK, Prime Minister? Are they involved? Could they be involved with the task force's arrival by sea, by any chance?"

"Possibly. The CIA have locked them down, so we have no access to them. I don't know how far the lockdown goes in Europe. Stewart, perhaps you can have a look, but don't involve the American Embassy. If you do that, you will alert the CIA. It is important we keep a lid on this in case it's pie in the sky. This could cause a cooling-off in our relationship. And no way can we use the word 'taskforce'. The carrier is just here on a goodwill visit, and that was all decided a long time ago; so it cannot be connected to the accident at Heathrow. Is that clear? If anybody is waylaid by the media, be honest: we have a plane crash at Heathrow, but we don't have any concise information and we are dealing with the accident in the normal way. You can ask them to check with their own circus if they want confirmation of what you say. All in all, we have a situation which has thrown everybody's agenda out of the window. And remember, the people – our people and the world – will be watching and expecting us to deal with this incident in a most professional way, as only the British can, so gentlemen, ladies, let's do it."

"Good morning, Prime Minister."

"General, I need to know, but on a don't-need-to-disclose basis – a few years ago we deployed the army, including tanks, at Heathrow, on an exercise to make a point and a show the world and the public our strength; do you recollect?"

"Yes, I do, Prime Minister. I was actually involved in the exercise and deployment. It was quite a good propaganda exercise for public relations. It improved general public awareness and provided reassurance, as I recall."

"General, can you tell me if you could do that again, and can you tell me how long it would take?"

"Prime Minister, we have kept some of the Warrior tanks in mothballs at the London barracks. We also have limited available manpower, but if required we could bring more from other bases fairly close, such as those in the West Country. I would need to know the numbers required, so I would want to know the reason. The last deployment was very easy and didn't really test our capabilities. It was mainly a defence deployment – not quite the same as an attack deployment."

"Thank you, General. Look – I'm honest with you – I don't know exactly what the requirement will be at this stage. It may be that we will only need you for crowd control; on the other hand, it may involve fighting. Can you tell me quickly how many tanks in working order you could deploy to Heathrow in the same manner as before at, say, twelve hours' notice?"

"Prime Minister, I can give you an answer within five hours."

"General, if you can make it in two and a half, I would appreciate that and I will put you on my Christmas list. Secretary, I want you to contact the head of MP at Scotland Yard and get him on the line."

"MP Commander, Scotland Yard, is on the line, Prime Minister."

"Hello, Commander. Have you any new information on Heathrow?"

"Prime Minister, we are not able to contact the base we have there, so we have issued instructions for the nearest local force to enter and evaluate and report back. We also have two helicopters on the fringe, but the fires are too intense to risk moving them closer. As yet we don't know the full extent of the damage or the area covered. I feel sure we'll bring the matter under control quickly, but first we need concrete information. Then we'll know which direction or method is the best to take."

"OK, Commander. We will need access into Heathrow for extra emergency vehicles, and to evacuate the casualties to local hospitals; so we need the approach roads as clear as possible. Can that be arranged?"

"Prime Minister, if you can specify the areas you need to access we can probably clear some roads, but not all. The traffic congestion is diabolical. It is totally gridlocked. The main entrance tunnel is blocked completely on both carriageways. We can't even get pedestrian access to the police station on the other side. We are impeded by the traffic volume on the approaches to the tunnel area. A team was sent on foot, but they reported that they can't get through. We are looking to see if we could put a helicopter down on the roof of one of the buildings or in a safe area. The helicopter crash could have been caused by the smoke affecting the helicopter's gyro, so we are proceeding with caution. If we can get a helicopter inside the perimeter, we will set up a surveillance centre to assist the emergency services. We are also in touch with the Army Medical Corps and we are looking for an area where we can set up a hospital unit. If we can do that within the airport, that will reduce the hospital transport problem."

"Commander, why do you think the army hospital is necessary?"

"Prime Minister, some time back I was assessing the hospital system the army has in Afghanistan and I thought the system would be useful if we had a disaster nearer home. Looking at the situation at Heathrow with fires burning and the area gridlocked, I am convinced that local hospitals will not be able to cope; a pop-up army hospital as near as possible to the crash site is the answer. It will reduce the pressure on local hospitals. The army is geared up to provide adequate facilities and personnel to deal with a sudden influx of casualties, such as might occur on a battlefield. Most hospitals aren't. We will also reduce the pressure on local roads. If a big plane has crashed, we could suddenly have 400 to 500 casualties, whereas most hospitals could probably cope with only ten or twenty at the most. Even the army will be stretched. We might be OK dealing with a few hundred men, but a few hundred men, women and children would be another matter. Unfortunately, the extent of the fire means we are not yet able to use helicopters to extract the casualties."

"OK, Commander, I can see your point. Update me on any developments."

"Prime Minister, the army general is on the line."

"OK, General. In addition to my first request, while you are sorting out your tank situation can you also find out what the army have regarding military hospitals – any mobile hospitals we could have at our fingertips – and what medical personal are available, say, in a 100-mile radius of Heathrow, just in case we need the extra help and support?

"Secretary, can you get on to the ambulance and hospital services and find out if they are geared up for this situation? Point out the traffic problems and ask them to liaise with the MP commander at Scotland Yard regarding access for ambulances in and out of Heathrow. It's no good if we have plenty of transport and personnel, but they can't reach the crash zone and attend to the casualties."

"Yes, Prime Minister."

"Stewart, I need your eyes and ears. You are probably more geared up to this than I am, so do you have any input, any ideas and advice?"

"Well, Prime Minister, I feel we have to cover every possibility. You probably noticed that some of the Cabinet members were not taking the situation very seriously, so their input is minimal. I have alerted the Members of Parliament for the affected areas. I think you need to contact them personally and insist they get involved. The same goes for members of the local councils. It would be good for public relations if we have one of our own Members at every hospital in the area. You can bet the media will have reporters and cameras there, so we can up our profile and show we are on top of the situation."

"Good thinking, Stewart! I don't expect the Deputy Prime Minister will have given that a thought, but I expect some of the opposition will be working out how to make the best they can from this incident."

"Prime Minister, air traffic control have now taken Heathrow off their radar list, so to speak."

"Secretary, what does that actually mean and how does it help the situation?"

"Prime Minister, we now don't have any planes hoping to land or take off at Heathrow in at least the next twenty-four hours. This will have a knock-on effect throughout the entire worldwide airspace. We have also been informed that there are probably two planes involved in the incident at Heathrow, not just one."

"Secretary, are you now saying we have a double crash scene? Have they crashed into each other?"

"Not sure, Prime Minister. We are waiting for more information, but air traffic control say they have two planes missing. They were both in the landing corridor and just two minutes apart, and they assume they are both on the ground at Heathrow, but nothing is certain. All contact has been lost with the control tower at Heathrow, but we think the second plane had entered the landing corridor and was transferred to Heathrow control tower for final approach instructions. It is feared that both planes crashed on landing."

"Secretary, does anyone know for sure where this other plane is?"

"No, Prime Minister, not yet. We are looking into it. It could have landed safely somewhere else. If it landed at Heathrow, as I believe, it cannot be seen because of the smoke."

"Could we have more than one crash site? Could they have crashed in different parts of the airport? We need to establish the facts, secretary – and fast, please. Do we know what effect the closure of Heathrow will have on the Americans, by any chance? What sort of problems will that cause them, and how can we alleviate those problems?"

"Prime Minister, I can say they will not be very pleased, by any stretch of the imagination. Of that I am sure. They have hundreds, probably thousands, of planes up in the air at any one time, and the ones heading for Heathrow will have had to divert elsewhere, not just in this country. Passengers will be dumped all over the place – all over the world – and I expect a vast number of the American passengers will be shouting the odds, as they usually do when things are not to their liking."

"Secretary, do we know how the other UK airports we have are coping with the extra loads of planes and people?"

"Not yet, Prime Minister. We are in touch with the Civil Aviation Authority and we are expecting some up-to-date information soon. We are lucky that the weather is OK. As far as I am aware none of the airports are closed due to fog or similar, and air traffic control have not reported any other problems."

"Stewart, you have some news which is good, I hope."

"I have been casting my ears around, Prime Minister, and have found out one of the reasons – probably the main reason – for the Americans locking down their bases. The lockdown is virtually worldwide and is in fact related to the Heathrow situation and the effect it is having on other airports. We think it is not because of the threat of terrorism, but to ensure they are kept open only for their own military access."

"Stewart, what exactly do you mean by that? Why would they need to lock down because of the situation at Heathrow?"

"Well, Prime Minister, the Pentagon issued the order for total lockdown because their military world strategy relies on the global access of their supply network to their armies to keep them going. As Heathrow is closed, they were concerned their own bases could end up being clogged up with passenger planes."

"That makes sense now. I see why Mike Sawyer was so concerned. He could see me insisting on using his bases in the UK as they have runways long enough to take the big passenger planes. He has probably had instructions from Head Office to avoid letting us use them as an alternative to Heathrow. Stewart, what do we actually know about these American bases? Have you ever been to one, by any chance?"

"No, Prime Minister, I've never been to one, but, oh yes, they are big. Everything American is big. Their home bases are usually as big as our small cities. They're more like complete towns than bases and they have many unknowns. Even the President doesn't know everything about them. Prime Minister, when you see the size and number of the transport planes the American air force use, you'll understand why they built such a large base in Afghanistan – Camp Bastion. From my own observation, when I was there, they have huge Galaxy transporter planes landing every two or three minutes almost every day of the year."

"I couldn't agree more with you, Stewart. On my own visit to Camp Bastion the base looked almost as big as Heathrow, if not bigger. They need a complete army just to protect the base, let alone the other bases out in the field, the feeding station and cold store. They are huge. They need about 10,000 meals a day, covering all types of diet for personnel of almost every religion; so they need to bring in supplies all the time, not just for that base but to distribute to other bases as well. The General told me they get through tons and tons of meat, vegetables and fruit each week. God help the sewage and water system! And that food all has to be brought in as there is no local produce available. If they couldn't get the planes to the base, their army would starve, or more likely just down weapons and go home. Add to that all the men and other supplies constantly in and out – ammunition, mail, medicine, fuel and body bags (empty and full) – and you have a full circus in action. It's like a small country."

"Hi, secretary. You have some more updates for me?"

"Not good, Prime Minister! Reports are coming in of large explosions and fireballs inside Heathrow, but still no precise details. The smoke cloud is dense and visible from miles away. It can even be seen from the top of the London Eye. We need some rain to damp down and clear the smoke."

"That has been one of my own personal concerns, Prime Minister."

"Stewart, can you explain your thinking, please?"

"Well, Prime Minister, when I heard the landing plane had probably hit the terminal my immediate concern was that it might have destroyed the infrastructure and wiped out the persons inside. There would have been other planes nearby, unloading and loading, and the ones loading would have been prepared for take-off, and would be full of fuel. Each plane, depending on the type and size, could be carrying roughly 50,000 gallons. That could explain the explosions and fireballs. There could be four or five or more loaded planes, so there could have been 500,000 gallons of high-octane fuel in the vicinity. That would explain the size of the conflagration."

"Gosh, Stewart, you are right! The planes they park in rows – a crashing plane would be like a bowling ball hitting the pins at the bowling alley. A plane could have hit the parked planes and the resulting fireball could have caused the devastation to the terminal. You could say that here was an accident waiting to happen. The whole thing could have been caused by bad parking by a pilot, rather than a plane falling out of the sky and hitting the terminal. That makes me think we should probably focus less on all our suggestions and worries and more on what we can gain from this. We need to start thinking about how we can gain party initiative and blight the other parties."

"I think, Prime Minister, we should let the situation roll as it is and let the other parties stay with it. They will be the ones who get the egg in the face if it turns out how we think it will. We can retain the high ground and adapt to the situation as it materialises. We can leave the 'told you so' inactive until needed. I have contacted the Air Ministry and asked if they could have some aerial photos taken by a high-flying reconnaissance plane. They say they will liaise with air traffic control to arrange a clear space. I have also asked my department if they can obtain satellite pictures."

"I agree, Stewart. We mustn't seem too smug. Just work on a need-to-know basis. Set up a 'good guy, bad guy' situation. Let them stew on that. We could gain from this. It would be good if we can get some photos – that would help us to assess the situation. I will have a chat with Cobra members and let them know our views. It might take some pressure off them and keep Mike Sawyer off our backs for a while, I might just give him something else to worry about if Heathrow is out of action for a while."

"Prime Minister, that would be brilliant. That will burn the phone lines to the Pentagon. The CIA will be worried sick that the President might say yes, so they will lobby anybody wearing trousers to make sure the President is fully aware of the grave consequences of saying yes. At the same time they will have to come up with an acceptable reason for him to say no. After all, he has always said he would help his allies."

"Stewart, I am looking forward to this. If he says no, we might be able to gain some concessions on other matters as a sweetener. I say bring on the CIA! Rock and roll!"

"Prime Minister, I can leak a snippet to the American Embassy as well, so Sawyer will get it from two directions. It will give it a bit more clout. He will then have to sweet-talk the ambassador *and* the President. I wouldn't mind betting we will have a quick visit from the ambassador asking us to reconsider before you talk to the President. Sawyer will probably have orders to sort it before that happens. Not only that, but the CIA would work out we could also ask the Queen to talk to the President. I mean, they got quite friendly on his last visit. America's First Lady's arm round the Queen went down very well in America with the Americans, if not at the Palace. It would be difficult for him to turn down Her Majesty's request."

"Hi, John. How's it going?"

"Secretary, not much news, though the news channel is continually open. The paper editors must be fuming as all they can see is flames and smoke. Visibility is bad. They would love to get closer and get pictures of piles of burning bodies or people running round burning and screaming. The police have arrested several reporters and cameramen who tried to get in. Just think: the first cameraman to get in will sell his pictures for thousands if he manages to avoid getting cremated at the same time."

"John, I am sure somebody will get in eventually. They can't keep the whole perimeter secure."

"No, secretary, it's a big area and there must be many ways in for service and delivery vehicles. Knowing the media, they will find a way to bribe their way in. I just hope that the first pictures will come from the security services. At least they will act with more dignity. Nearby hospitals are full of cameramen waiting for the first casualties to arrive. Just think: some poor victims could turn up badly injured and be surrounded by flashing lights and have microphones pushed into their faces and journalists screaming for answers. I don't expect there will be many policemen on hand to assist."

"Gosh, John, you are so right! I will bring this up with the Prime Minister. Prime Minister, if I can have a minute . . ."

"Secretary, you look like you have a problem?"

"Sir, I have just pinpointed a cause for concern – a major concern."

"Yes, secretary, carry on – what is worrying you?"

"Prime Minister, the hospitals which are awaiting the first

casualties are thronged with reporters and cameramen, and the police are nowhere to be seen. I have spoken to the MP commander at Scotland Yard, but they have no spare officers. All their available officers are deployed at Heathrow. They are bringing more officers from other forces; but that will take time, and time is something we have very little of."

"How can we help them, secretary? What actually can we do?"

"We need to provide the hospitals with more security. If and when the casualties arrive, they could be mugged, swamped and traumatised by the media. They could end up having heart attacks, and God knows what else may happen!"

"Secretary, don't the hospitals have their own security men to cope with this type of situation?"

"Yes, hospitals do have security personnel, but usually just one or two, Prime Minister. They usually rely on the local police if extra help is required. The problems they usually have are normally drink-related, that sort of thing. If there is a serious incident, then the police are called, but the police are not available at the moment."

"OK, secretary, contact the chiefs of the concerned hospitals, explain the situation and ask them to maximise their security. We will discuss extra funding after this is all sorted. Make it clear that the safety of the patients is a government priority. And pass all this on to the Health Secretary. Get her involved and ask her to report to me every hour – is that clear?"

"I will arrange that straight away Prime Minister."

"Prime Minister, I've just had your secretary giving me a specific order. Is this your doing, by any chance?"

"Yes, Health Secretary. He was carrying out my specific instructions. Do you have a report for me?"

"Yes, Prime Minister, I do. I have only just arrived from the dentist, so I am not feeling in the mood to start rushing around making phone calls and sending messages."

"Health Secretary, I am sorry about the dentist, but we have a much more pressing problem. Have you been following the news from Heathrow?"

"I've seen only what is on the television, so I am not fully up to date quite yet."

"OK, sit down and I will put you in the picture. This is a major incident. We don't know just how many casualties there are, but we need to be ready to handle a large number. We don't just sit back and wait till we know the numbers. We can't just wait till they arrive, then open the door; we may find the door is not wide enough. All the hospitals local to Heathrow are on alert, but that also means they are covered with the media circus. Imagine for a moment that when you left the dentist you had to run the gauntlet of twenty reporters and cameramen. Imagine you came out on a stretcher with part of your jaw missing. We need to try to prevent journalists from harassing the injured, so I want you to take charge of the hospitals. Use any resources required so after this fact the party will be praised and not ridiculed. Our first priority is the hospitals' security. The police can't help. Get extra manpower. Make use of the other parties; make sure the press secretary is on the case. See if she can obtain passenger lists from the airlines. Don't assume it is just one airline involved. Who knows, one of the casualties could be a VIP, who could already be an RIP. Any problems, let us know, but deal with it decisively. Use the media for our benefit and don't allow the opposition to use it for theirs. Any questions?"

"Gosh, Prime Minister! I am sorry. OK, I wasn't aware of the gravity of the situation. Toothache or not, be assured that I will be on the case forthwith."

"Good. Keep me informed. I will ask Stewart to liaise with you. He is getting to grips with it all. He is a good spokesman and he gives good advice and help, so make use of him."

"The General is on the line, Prime Minister."

"General, you have good news for me, I hope?"

"Prime Minister, we will have six Warrior tanks ready to roll in three hours. I am in talks with the MP commander at Scotland Yard regarding traffic, and we have discussed the best way for us to reach Heathrow. The fifteen or so miles normally take us less than an hour, but we will be hampered by traffic. I have also alerted several of our bases in the West Country to be ready should we need to deploy additional men and I've requested all medical staff and facilities to be available if required. By road is not the ideal way to transport casualties, but it's our best option at the moment. Also, Prime Minister, I have contacted Hereford and asked them to stand by at RAF Northolt in case they are needed. It's just a precaution."

"Did you get that, Stewart? What's the Hereford connection? Is it what I think, by any chance?"

"Well, Prime Minister, I imagine he was referring to the SAS. They are the only regiment based at Hereford, and I know they have an office at RAF Northolt, as they do at Scotland Yard. I imagine the General is covering himself just in case."

"That's my feeling too, Stewart. It's good for him, and good that we don't actually appear to know – but we do know, if you follow my thinking. His discretion works in our favour. I mean, he never actually mentioned the SAS. I expect he assumes we know what he means, but do we? I don't think we should make any assumptions or ask questions which could be used against us at a later date."

"That is something we need to conceal, Prime Minister. If that got out, the media would have a field day and we could have catastrophic countrywide panic as well as the Americans jumping up and down. I just hope the Americans haven't got a spy camping outside or a spy in the sky at the Hereford base. They might notice unusual movement or increased activity around the base."

"At least, Stewart, if the balloon goes up, we can appear to be surprised. But we'll also be prepared. The opposition parties won't have a clue and they'll look pretty foolish. Ah, Stewart, I want you to keep tabs on the General. If the SAS have to get involved, bypass him and deal with them directly. Get your information straight from the horse's mouth. We don't want the General taking all the glory, but he can take all the criticism and flak that comes as a result of any mistakes."

"Prime Minister, I have had a conversation with the Shepherd at Hereford."

"The Shepherd, Stewart? What are we up to now – looking after flocks of sheep?"

"Well, Prime Minister, quite often we could do with having a shepherd and his dog in Parliament, as the opposition parties behave like a flock of sheep at times, all following one another one minute and going astray the next. We could sometimes do with a dog to round them up and put them in order. But the Shepherd at Hereford is the main operations officer. Don't ask his real name or rank, because they never use real names. He is aware of the situation, and he will have his operations office at an undisclosed location close to Heathrow within the next couple of hours."

"OK, Stewart, I understand – nudge nudge (wink wink). We don't need to know. The secret service will handle the nasty stuff if it appears; if it doesn't, they will disappear and no one will ever be the wiser. I hope they remember whose side they are on."

"Secretary, I am taking a break. I will be in my flat if you need me, but keep me informed."

"Yes, Prime Minister. Rest assured. My finger is on your pulse as well as mine. I will inform you of any developments that require your immediate attention."

CHAPTER TWO

"Hello, Jayne darling. I must say I am very glad to see you again."

"Richard, I am glad you still remember my name and who I am. You look very tired."

"I know it's been one hell of a day so far and I haven't seen you since breakfast. It's probably been the longest single day of my life so far, but even so I could never forget you or who you are. It doesn't matter how difficult the job, the day, life is, you are always deep inside my mind and thoughts."

"Well, we knew right from the beginning, before we moved in, that our way of life would totally change, and it wouldn't be just like a nine-to-five normal office job with free weekends; but I didn't think it would be a twenty-four-hours-a-day, seven-days-a-week job. We didn't expect it to be 365 days a year, and nights as well."

"Oh, Jayne darling, I have to be honest with you if nobody else: it's a bad job. There are very few pleasures or rewards. Everything I do or say is scrutinised to the very last detail – not because anybody wants to heap praise, but because they want to find a mistake, a chink in my armour. Every simple little error they make into a major fault."

"Richard, I know the feeling. Oh, boy, I know that feeling! It is the same for me. The other mothers I meet seem so nice, so friendly; yet I know deep down they are not pleased for me, and pleased for my amazing lifestyle. They are envious, and they probably hate me for it. They smile to my face, but my back has lately become like a pincushion."

"I know, Jayne, it is hard to be happy. Being with you is so special, but I can't fully enjoy our time together; I can't switch off like I used to. I can't pop down to the takeaway for a simple meal. I can't move an inch without someone knowing. I just want to shut the door, curl up on the sofa with you, watch some silly film, enjoy a drink, even get a bit merry, have a laugh, shut the door and sleep till the morning."

"Richard, I ask myself a hundred times a day why? Why did you want to be a Prime Minister? What can you achieve for yourself and for your family? Is it really worth giving up your life, giving up your very own existence, just for a few years? Then you will be pushed to one side and forgotten about. I was talking to Marjorie the other day, and she had a good point. She said, 'When we move out, and return to the fold, we will only be remembered for the bad happenings.' Nobody will ever remember the good you achieved. That will be remembered as someone else's achievement. Marjorie also added that the word on the street is that you, my darling, are someone who says everything but achieves nothing! I told her that was unfair and disrespectful, especially considering the enormous time and effort you put in every single day; and I know better than most how hard you work."

"Jayne darling, you are so right. I do envy Stewart so much. Losing the election and not having to do the job would have seemed bad at the time, but not any more. I should not really feel like this, but in my heart I feel that this Heathrow business will be my Waterloo. There is no way I can put the fire out by myself; I am having to take charge of a situation I in fact have no control over. I don't have the knowledge or experience to cope with a large-scale disaster. I am a very small pawn on a huge chessboard. Before I just had the Cabinet round me, but now I have the police, the fire service, hospitals, the ambulance service, Health & Safety, airports, air traffic control, the army, the air force, the navy and every bloody service on this planet. Oh, and let's not forget the Americans! I mean, just look at Downing Street – the hub, the so-called throbbing hub of this country. We have a major disaster on our hands and the place is empty. We have a few almost retired civil servants passing pieces of paper on to me – they are doing the best they can, but they are just in the dark like me. The Cabinet members have left the ship and will keep their distance until it is safe to return – 'safe' meaning they can't be blamed for any misdoings. The opposition parties are sitting on the fence, waiting to know which side to get down on and hoping – not that the danger to the public will pass with minimum casualties and hardship but that the danger will inflict the greatest-possible damage on me and my party."

"Oh, Richard, I've not seen you like this before. Perhaps Heathrow *will* turn out to be your Waterloo, but I am sure, with all my heart, you will come out as a Wellington, not a Napoleon. Just make sure you don't walk around with your hand tucked into your shirt. After all, I want to be a Jayne and not a Josephine – and remember, I am available every single night you need me."

"Thank you, darling. You will always be my Jayne, the loveliest and most amazing women I have ever known. That's why I married you. You know something, whenever we are making love you always have your eyes open; you never close them. I can see it means just as much to you as to me, and it is so exciting and pleasurable as we orgasm together. And that is just the beginning! We don't roll over and go to sleep! We spend a long time just looking into each other's eyes with total satisfaction. Some time back I was speaking with a journalist after the election, and, darling, he told me his views. What he said didn't mean much to me then, but it means a whole lot more now. He said, 'It takes us men several meetings and many days to come up with a solution to a problem; yet if we just went down the pub and asked our wives to sort it out, they could have an afternoon tea party and sort the whole thing out in a couple of hours and still have time for a chat and a look at the new fashion magazines and pick the kids up from school. And they would come up with a better solution than we men could!'"

"Darling, I couldn't agree more. We women can see right through you men. The coalition is just one big joke – always was and always will be. Can you see Alex Ferguson being happy if Manchester United went through a whole season only drawing or losing, but never winning, a game. I mean, come on! These days

Parliament is more like a gunfight at the OK Corral with everybody firing blanks. The Liberal Party are showing the public that they are incapable of running the country by themselves, and the best job in the kitchen for them is the washing-up; just don't let them do the cooking. They are good at eating the cakes, but no good at baking. When you think back to the Oliver Cromwell film, when he marched into Parliament and threw all the idiot Parliament members out and replaced them with good common-sense people – oh, if we could do that again!"

"Oh, Jayne, you will have to build an army of petticoats soldiers to do that. I can just imagine a session in Parliament being interrupted by an army of women, marching in waving their rolling pins, and ordering their husbands home for their tea, or to look after the kids. Do you think we might get our life back sometime in the future?"

"Richard, I can't predict the future, by any stretch of my imagination. We have to get through this crisis first, and hope we come up smelling of roses; otherwise the future is bleak, very bleak. This crisis could cause us to lose the next general election, of that I am sure – not that I would cry if we had to move out. Actually, I probably would, but I often think just how good it would be to have our life back and be normal again. We have to believe there will be life after 10 Downing Street."

Suddenly there was a buzzing noise!

"That will be for you, I expect. I did warn you not to have that intercom fitted. I did think at the time it would become a weight round your neck, but I never said so in so many words."

CHAPTER THREE

"Secretary, you have some news?"

"Prime Minister, thank you for answering. Sir, we have further information."

"OK, secretary, I will be with you in just a minute." The Prime Minister turned to his wife: "Well, darling, you were right as usual. I will have to leave you again. Just in case I am not back by bedtime, I will say goodnight. I think this will be going on for a long time yet, so you go to bed without me. Hopefully, I'll join you for breakfast, at least. Right, secretary, I am back with you, all ears. What news do you have?"

"We have located the missing plane – well, we think it is the missing plane. No one has actually been able to say for definite that it is the one, but I am reasonably sure."

"Well, where has it got to and, secretary, why hasn't it been verified yet?"

"Well, the MP at Scotland Yard have been getting hundreds of phone calls from the public, including the usual plane spotters around the perimeter. We've put together all the information, and it appears the first plane was coming in to land as normal, but before touchdown there was an explosion from one wing and it slewed off sideways in the direction of Terminal 5 and crashed. Had the wind been in the opposite direction, the planes would have been landing the other way and probably crashed into Terminal 1 or Terminal 2. The next plane came in as normal, touched down then ran into a wall of flames on the runway – probably a spillage from the crashed plane. The plane was engulfed and disappeared from sight. It probably went through the wall of fire and came to a stop on the other side. It was not seen aborting and taking off again. No further information has been received. All the phone calls we received after that just confirmed what I have just told you, so the MP commander at Scotland Yard thinks this information is conclusive – that is, two planes have landed and probably crashed at Heathrow, and almost certainly it happened as I have described."

"Stewart, have you any other thoughts on this?"

"Well, Prime Minister, we are no further forward with bringing this crisis to an end. It is a complex and daunting situation for the emergency services as well as the police. I wonder what caused the problems at the entrance tunnel. The crash is not at that end of Heathrow. An immense number of persons are caught up in this – not just the immediate crash victims, but all the persons who live near Heathrow, the persons who have just stopped for a look, the persons who work at Heathrow, the persons waiting to board and the ones waiting to take off. We have a gridlock of plane traffic on the ground and people in the terminals. The local hotels, however, will do well."

"I see. OK, Stewart. You paint a very depressing picture. We have a major disaster to deal with, affecting a large part of the city, not just the airport. We need to clear the area of persons who are not required to be there so that the emergency services can deal with the victims. We might need every available hospital bed, doctor and nurse we can find, and we might have to go further afield than the London area. The hospitals could be totally overloaded with burns victims. On my last hospital visit I saw just how much nursing a severely burnt person needs. Some may have to be treated at specialist hospitals. Even if we don't have a great number of casualties, we might not have the resources to cope with them adequately. Do we have any idea how many persons there are normally in Heathrow during the day?"

"Not off the top of my head, Prime Minister – probably a few thousand passengers, maybe more, and probably a few thousand airport employees. I will try to get a head count. We have not yet had any passenger lists from the airlines. My department is contacting where the planes took off from as this end we have not been able to locate any one from the airlines who can give us the information we require. It makes me wonder if when they built the new Terminal 5 they also incorporated wiring and cable connections to all the other terminals. I don't expect they would have imagined that they could lose a complete terminal building just like that – especially as it consists of three buildings, not just one. Hopefully, only one of the buildings is affected, and that could be just one of the two Terminal 5 satellite buildings."

"Surely, Stewart, all the cabling and connections would be underground, so they should not be affected. When this is all sorted we will be able to implement new safety methods based on experience gained in this crisis. In future we must make sure we have effective backup in all areas."

"That's right, Prime Minister. Mind you, what are the chances of having two plane crashes on the same day at nearly the same time and location? Well, I very much doubt if it will happen again. New safety measures will probably be a very costly safeguard – a reassurance to travellers. . . . Prime Minister, I think we may have good news."

"Thank God for that, secretary."

"Yes, the MP commander at Scotland Yard has established contact with personnel on site at Terminal 1. There is no contact with Terminal 5 yet. They have informed us that the airport is in total pandemonium. Vast numbers of persons are flooding out, abandoning the terminals from all directions. Numerous persons have collapsed, and there are reports of coughing and spluttering. The terminal buildings are in darkness, and fumes and smoke are bellowing out everywhere. Firemen using breathing apparatus have been bringing persons out of the dark depths and collapsing themselves with exhaustion. We have no details of casualties yet. The chief fire officer has set up a command centre and is liaising with all the other emergency services. He is having to bring in firefighting personnel and appliances from Gatwick and the surrounding areas, including London. He said the Terminal 1 building has two major incident areas. No structural damage has been reported, though flames and smoke are coming up the lift and stairways from the Underground station. The lifts and escalators are not working, so they have not been able to gain entry to the station. They are trying to gain access from one of the other terminals to tackle the fire. They think they can send an appliance via the low-level road access or the Underground tunnels. The terminal windows facing the runway have been blown in at all levels. Smoke and fumes are billowing from Terminal 5, which he identifies as the main crash scene, but they have not been able to set up a command post at Terminal 5 owing to lack of available manpower. He has sent a team to look and evaluate. Planes parked adjacent to Terminals 1 and 2 have been damaged, but they have safely evacuated some, if not all, of the passengers. They have not yet been able to give us any details about casualties. He says they need more help – a hell of a lot more personnel to help with the evacuation process and to treat the injured. We shall need all the oxygen supplies, doctors, nurses, blankets, stretchers and ambulances we can locate in order to assist persons suffering from burns and smoke inhalation. He says they are expecting the same problems at other terminals, particularly Terminal 5. He has also informed the MP commander at Scotland Yard that people living near the airport should be told to shut their windows as the smoke is very toxic, especially for persons who already have health problems. He has not yet been able to give any information about the possible leaking fuel or the reason for the explosions, but they are now short of foam and he does not know what has happened to most of the airport firefighting appliances. He thinks they might be at Terminal 5 tackling the blaze there. He has pointed out that burning kerosene cannot be extinguished with just water. Water turns to red-hot, scalding, suffocating steam. Kerosene is normally dealt with using foam; and as kerosene would not normally be expected to enter a building the terminals have no automatic foam system."

"Secretary, can you contact the General, please? General, can you mobilise your tanks and make your way to Heathrow Terminal 1? We need you to oversee the evacuation procedure. In a similar way the American National Guard will deploy in a disaster area and assist the emergency services. You may need to equip your troops with stretchers and first-aid kits instead of guns, and mobilise any medical teams you have available – especially ones that can help with burns and smoke inhalation. Please keep me updated as you proceed."

"Stewart, I want you to act as an information coordinator. You will need to liaise with the General, the MP commander at Scotland Yard and the command centre and emergency services at Heathrow. I have instructed the General to take his tanks there. Fire engines and ambulances are what we need most, but the tanks give an air of authority. They will reassure the public that we are in control of the situation."

"I'm already working on that, Prime Minister; I'm also keeping tabs on the Americans. At the moment all seems to be working well. The lot I am not doing so well with are the opposition – especially the shadow Cabinet. I can sense they are plotting to gain the high ground if we trip over."

"Oh, yes, and I have noticed how often the Deputy Prime Minister is keeping an unusually safe distance. You know, I sometimes think if I fell down and faked a heart attack, the Liberals would pick him up and race into Parliament to get him sworn in. I expect he would look totally vacant and bewildered and in pain, just as he always does when asked to do anything."

"Maybe so, Prime Minister, but he is good at making the tea and passing the cakes round. I just hope he is still here for the next general election as he is our best ticket to win. He makes you look so good and the others so bad. I find it so reassuring the way the Liberal and Labour Members are becoming so friendly. They are both hoping they can join forces and become the next coalition government. So long as they keep Peter and Paul up front that will convince the public not to vote for them. I mean, neither looks capable as a Prime Minister, and they look even worse together."

"You are right there, Stewart. I would have been worried if they had picked the other brother, Terry. He would have caused us more concern. He looks the part. But as long as the silly brother is there I am not too worried. He gets on well with Peter. They are both the same. They probably both like making the tea and would look good as a double act."

"Prime Minister, at times you sound so cynical, but you are so right. Anyway, back to what is in hand. It might be an idea to put one of our own in on the ground at Terminal 1, so we will be well informed of developments as they happen. No doubt the media will be sniffing around – plenty of interviews and picture-taking going on. As we know, good news doesn't sell papers; so I expect they will be digging with dirty shovels. I worked out some time back that on their word processors the grammar corrector has been fiddled with so that it ensures the wording is totally out of context, and no matter how you answer their question the printed version is always different. The grammar fiddler is probably an accountant; so the printed words will be the most damaging, to create the best sales and make the most money. If you ever want an honest answer, never ask a journalist or an accountant."

"Gosh, yes, Stewart! Have you noticed – I expect you have – when incorrect information is printed in big letters on the front page the apology is printed in small type somewhere else and the editor says that is just because of lack of space? Hogwash! A decent honest person would print the apology on the front page, but you won't find the word 'honest' or 'truth' in the tabloids' dictionary."

"Prime Minister, sir."

"Yes, secretary?"

"Prime Minister, I think Heathrow should be designated a major disaster area."

"Secretary, are you saying the problem may be worse than we already think?"

"Prime Minister, we know already that there are far too many people involved for the normal emergency services and police force to cope with. It is totally unprecedented. We just don't have anybody in total control. We need more generals and more Indians. All the services are working flat out, but we need a more coordinated approach. It's as though we are trying to use small corks to plug a large hole. It simply won't work. Imagine filling Wembley Stadium with casualties and having just half a dozen doctors, nurses, policemen and firemen to cope with them. It just won't work. The smoke is hampering us. We still don't know the extent of the damage, so we haven't been able to implement the necessary operational procedure to bring the situation under control. On top of that, road traffic accidents near the airport are being blamed on the smoke."

"Thank you, secretary."

"Stewart, we need to include more Cabinet members, and we need to draft in more help. Let's look at Heathrow as the scene of a battle. The army should be more involved. They probably have personnel and vehicles gathering dust that could be put to good use. In the past we have often deployed army firefighters with their Green Goddess vehicles – and don't forget the RAF. They have personnel and equipment for dealing with plane crashes."

"Prime Minister, some of that equipment is in mothballs. It might take so long to get it into operation that it will come too late."

"Stewart, I've just thought of another area that could be problematic. If the death toll is high, we will need to set up a temporary mortuary. Think of the nightmare if the passengers on just one plane are killed! We will have to be seen to be able to cope. And ask British Telecom to set up some help-and-advice phone lines. Make sure they understand that persons from many different countries with different languages may want to use the service."

"Prime Minister, I was thinking the same regarding possible casualties. Ideally we need to take over a large cold store. I will ask the Food Secretary to organise something."

"Make sure, Stewart, that the Food Secretary is very discreet. I don't want anyone in that department to blab to the media. I am sure there are persons in most departments who are in the pay of the media. Far too often I read what is to happen or has already happened before I am actually told by my own advisers. I am sure if the media knew we were looking for a large mortuary, they would have a field day. At times like this we can learn from the Americans. They have considerable knowledge and experience of dealing with large numbers of dead bodies – they have been doing it since Custer's Last Stand."

"I agree, Prime Minister, but I think we should wait till we know more before we involve the Americans; and don't forget that ours is an older country than theirs. Britain was fighting wars before America was born."

"That may be so, Stewart, but most of our wars took place in someone else's country. What would be the general reaction of the British to large numbers of casualties on our own soil? In case of war, would we be able to defend the beaches? Whose side would the immigrants be on? Would they just sit it out and join the winners? And the politicians – would we all join hands or would we swap sides? We don't yet know how many, if any, Americans are among the casualties. It would only need one congressman or film star to be injured or dead and we will have the complete Stars and Stripes media circus to cope with as well."

"I see your point, Prime Minister, but we got through the Blitz. Perhaps we can get through this crisis in the same way."

"The problem with that, Stewart, is that the London Blitz was a very long time ago. People are very different now. I don't know if people will pull together as they did in the Blitz, and it may be more like dog eat dog."

CHAPTER FOUR

"Prime Minister, I must switch on the TV. There is something you must see. It happened just a few minutes ago and we have recorded it."

"Hello, people of Britain. Who am I? you might ask. My name is not important; what is important is that you watch my broadcast to the nation which will begin in thirty minutes. I hope your government will be switched on and ready to take notice."

"Is that it, Secretary – just that? Do we know what this is all about?"

"Prime Minister, we don't know who that man is or even where the broadcast came from. We have not been able to find out anything. We don't know if it's from the UK or another country, if it was genuine or a sick hoax."

"Stewart, it was not our friends at the CIA by any chance – what do you think?"

"Prime Minister, I don't think it was American-related. The man looks a bit tribal, like someone from Afghanistan."

"Secretary, see if MI5 and MI6 can identify this man. Who is he and where has he come from? We have no idea what he is up to, but in thirty minutes we will hear his next broadcast – that is if he broadcasts again? Secretary, do we know if that message was broadcast in any other country?"

"Prime Minister, it was probably worldwide. According to the BBC, he has somehow hacked into several channels. The BBC say they have their boffins looking into it at the moment, trying to locate the source."

"Stewart, have you any further news?"

"Prime Minister, I have just been talking to Mike Sawyer. The CIA also saw the broadcast and are trying to identify the man as well. Sawyer agrees that he looks like an Afghan, though he has no beard or headgear, which you would expect if he was a high-ranking Afghan. He looks more Western. Mike also pointed out that he appears to have very blue eyes – again a Western characteristic. Mike also said that at first bounce they have been unable to identify him."

"Stewart, I never took any notice of his features. Is what Mike said true? Can you confirm his description? And what's this 'first bounce'? What does that mean exactly?"

"Prime Minister, the bounce is when they put the man's picture on their computer system, which can quickly compare him with everyone else on their database. It's a database of undesirables. And, yes, we have blown up the television picture and had a good look at his features. We can confirm Mike's evaluation, and, yes, he looks Western judging by eye colour but not by skin colour; he could be a Westerner who has spent some time living in the Indian continent."

"Stewart, do you think we might be on that CIA database? That looks like very good news, then, if he has not been identified by their first bounce. What do you think?"

"Not necessarily, Prime Minister. He could be still be a problem, but not yet known – a sort of mole. He could be the top man in an organisation, but to the world he could just appear as an innocent goatherd. He might never have appeared at any gatherings, so has escaped detection and hasn't been killed by an American drone. He may usually communicate by word of mouth, and never use the Internet or phone system. When he speaks he probably looks down with his hands on his forehead, to thwart lip-readers. The Americans are working on decoding a system of sign language used by Middle Eastern terrorists. Apparently just tapping a finger or fingers in a sequence is a way of communicating. A terrorist needs only a few words or a few letters to understand the message – he doesn't use the Oxford Dictionary, as we do."

"Stewart, point taken. It seems as though we will be waiting in limbo for the next instalment to arrive! It makes me shudder. Were the CIA right about Heathrow? Have we missed the start of the game? Is the ball in play? Are we the failed receivers? I am thinking like an American football player."

"I don't think so, Prime Minister. We have had no actual proof that we have a terrorist incident at Heathrow. I am sure somebody would have noticed if there was a group of mad different-looking men racing round on camels or donkeys, screaming and firing guns, and throwing bombs. I think we can discount that theory until we have concrete information to the contrary."

"Secretary, do we have everything in place to react quickly, in case this broadcast happens and there is a serious terrorist threat?"

"Prime Minister, we have all our eyes and ears covering every possible avenue and location."

"Hello, Great Britain."

"He's bang on time."

"Hello, Prime Minister. I trust you are listening and recording this broadcast, and I expect you have your so-called excellent security departments busy trying to trace my origin. On no account should you switch off this transmission as that would have very serious consequences for all the people of the United Kingdom."

"Everything still running, Secretary? Are we all geared up?"

"All systems operating, Prime Minister. We are trying to trace the source."

"Prime Minister, in order to save you time and effort, I will now reveal my location and purpose."

The picture on the TV screen changed as the recording camera panned round. The speaker was sitting down and didn't have an AK47 or rocket launcher across his knees. Neither was he wearing a black mask or turban.

"As you can see, I am sitting comfortably at a very special desk – the very desk your queen sits at when she does her

Christmas broadcast to the nation. Yes, Prime Minister, I am very close to you at this very moment. I am actually sitting in a room at Buckingham Palace, and look who is sitting here with me. It's your royal family."

"Jesus Christ Almighty! Stewart, how can he be there? Secretary, quick – you must get things moving pronto. Contact the palace and get confirmation that this is not real. For God's sake, I am having a bad nightmare! This can't be happening. Tell me it's some university students or kids playing a prank."

"So, Prime Minister, as you can see, your royal family are in good health and have not been harmed in any way. People of Britain, I can assure you that no harm will come to your royal family at our hands; any harm to them will be inflicted entirely by your Prime Minister and his government. Now, Prime Minister, we know you will not negotiate with us, and we respect that. You have no way to communicate with us and this broadcast is the only way we will communicate with you. We don't need to ask any questions; we will tell you our requirements and instructions, which you must carry out. We will not negotiate."

"Secretary, what do you have? Talk to me."

"Prime Minister, at present there is no communication or link with the palace. Everything is a total blank. We don't even have a mobile-phone connection. We will keep trying. We have other plans in motion. I will come back to you if we have any more news."

"Prime Minister, in the last few minutes you made two rather stupid futile attempts to storm the palace. We have swiftly and completely dealt with both attempts!"

"Stewart, do you know what he means? What the hell is he talking about?"

"No, I don't have a clue, Prime Minister. I will try to find out."

"Prime Minister, listen carefully. If there are any further attempts by persons to enter the palace or the palace grounds by foot or air, we will say you have declared war and we shall wipe out all the persons within the palace. We shall

also reduce the entire building to rubble and dust. People of Britain, if your Prime Minister destroys your monarchy and buildings, you yourselves can try him in your courts for an act of treason."

"News, Stewart – what do you have?"

"Prime Minister, the MP at Scotland Yard sent two CO19 cars [armed response vehicles] straight away when they knew the location, but they have lost contact. Also the army launched their highly trained automatic rapid-response unit from Wellington Barracks, which is only 250 yards from the palace, but they also have lost contact at the moment."

(The British army has a constant presence adjacent to Buckingham Palace to provide guards during the day. There is also a trained unit on constant standby at Wellington Barracks to tackle any emergency at the palace. Their training is based on situations that could happen, but nothing like this had ever happened before. The unit had only ever carried out practice drills, and had not deployed for real-life combat emergencies. A certain amount of complacency existed, and so the rapid-response unit did not have the knowledge and experience to deal with any out-of-the-normal situations. The army's security role is to patrol the palace area inside the boundaries; the Metropolitan Police is in charge outside the palace grounds.)

"Stewart, get the MP commander at Scotland Yard to set up a cordon round the palace. Nobody is to enter – I mean nobody. I don't want some lost tourist wandering in or somebody turning up to read the gas or electric meters, or any delivery drivers accidentally triggering a total wipeout."

"Also, Prime Minister, at present all the lighting inside and outside the building is on. If you cut the power, the loss of voltage will automatically trigger the detonators. We have no qualms about dying ourselves. People of Britain, if your government behaves in the correct way, nobody will lose their lives. We are here to bring peace and not to make a war. We will broadcast our requirements in fifteen minutes' time, provided that your government, your Prime Minister, has not murdered us and your royal family and reduced

Buckingham Palace to a pile of rubble and dust."

"Christ almighty! My God! Oh, hell! For God's sake! My God! Jesus Christ! My God! God Almighty! Right, everybody, we've got fifteen minutes to use wisely. Information, information, data, data, data! Has anybody identified this lunatic yet? Is he real? Where has he come from? What the hell is MI5 doing? How the hell can he walk into this country and just walk into the palace like that? What the bloody hell is Border Control doing? Not only that, but does anybody know how many terrorists are now in the palace or in the bloody country? Secretary, convene Parliament. We need every voice. I want advice. Get the General and all his staff here now. I want a person with direct connection with the MP commander at Scotland Yard standing by my shoulder. Get the head of MI5 here straight away. Find out where those two patrol units are and find out where that army rapid-response unit is. Make sure they are not in the palace grounds. If the terrorists observe soldiers running round, they will detonate. God, I don't want to go down in history as the Prime Minister who caused the country to lose its monarchy. Secretary, you have some up-to-date information?"

"Prime Minister, I have contacted the head of the Royal Protection department and instructed him to locate and ensure the security of royal family members not at the palace. Use the marines if necessary. At least the princes, William and Harry, have some combat experience. Also the MP commander at Scotland Yard has had no contact with the protection officers at the palace by phone or radio."

"Thank you, secretary. Stewart, do you have an update for me?"

"Yes, Prime Minister, the MP at Scotland Yard have created a cordon round the palace and set up a command centre. That means they have withdrawn some support at Heathrow. Also they have set up a camera. I will switch on this monitor so you can see. There are the two patrol cars, both upside down and totally burnt wreckage. The MP at Scotland Yard think there are bodies inside. They are trying to locate a mobile camera that they could send in to look. I have told them not to take any chances – probably best to leave well alone and not enter the palace space. That's where the non-negotiable treaty falls down. We can't contact the terrorists, so we can't access the palace grounds and remove any bodies. We have scanned all the grounds, but there is no sign of the army unit. There is an ambulance by the main entrance and a brown UPS delivery van parked by the gatehouse, but no signs of life anywhere. The MP commander at Scotland Yard is trying to obtain a thermal-imaging camera. Perhaps that will give us some idea how many persons are in the palace. We might learn exactly where the terrorists are."

"Stewart, helicopters – media! Jesus! God alive! We need to make certain that the bloody media don't find a helicopter to fly over the palace taking pictures. If the terrorists hear a helicopter they will think the SAS are coming in from the roof and detonate. Get hold of the General. Get him to set up a ring of guns and rockets round the palace. If a helicopter turns up, shoot the thing down. I don't want a film of Buckingham Palace blowing up appearing on the TV. Oh, God! I just remembered that American film when the terrorist broadcast a picture of the White House being blown up! That was just a fake – I don't want ours to be the real thing! And make sure the MP at Scotland Yard haven't got a police helicopter hanging about. I am getting paranoid about bloody helicopters now! I've just thought – what if a cat or a dog triggers the detonation! Oh my God, what about the royal corgis! I never noticed them in the broadcast, did you?"

"No, Prime Minister. I am not sure if they are at the palace; but, if so, I am sure they will be all right. They're probably shut away somewhere safe!"

"You know, Stewart, he never mentioned the palace staff. They are very clever, not letting us contact them, as they don't have to answer any questions we come up with. We have no way of knowing if the staff are alive and well. Stewart, that's another thing – staff. Make sure the men in the cordon keep an eye out for any distressed family members of the palace staff. Having seen the TV, they could turn up and rush in to try to rescue their loved ones."

"OK, everyone, settle down. Just stay calm. The broadcast is about to start, if he is on time."

"Hello again, people of Britain. We can report that we are all well at the palace, and, as you can see, your Royal Family are well and safe. We have decided to give you your royal family back, but, yes, we have a condition. As you are fully aware, over the past years your governments have acted with total – and I mean total – disregard for the safety and well-being of other people. They have carried out numerous atrocities, including the murdering of men, women and innocent children, with bombs and bullets in many countries round the world. Your Prime Ministers – your very own elected leaders – have plunged you into wars you can never win. They have used lies and deceit solely to improve their own standing with the Americans. They have done so with very little regard for you or the interests of this country. So, people of Britain, even if you have voted for and supported them, we don't have any grievance with you. Our grievance is only with your government. If you wish to have your royal family safely back, your governments will have to comply with a simple and straightforward request! We will produce a list of names of men we want to see. Why? Well, we want to ask them a series of questions, and we want to transmit to you their answers so that we can prove they have not behaved in a humane way. Then you can make your own judgment on them, and the entire world will be able to observe just how honest the leaders of the UK are. We require all the men on the list to come to the palace and walk in. When they are all here we will release the royal family. We will then broadcast the answers. The men are all government men. We shall then hand ourselves over to the British people and have our day in a British court. British people, you have my word that you will have the government men back alive. Our interrogation will be fair and honest – unlike

their interrogation of my brothers, we will not inflict any torture to extract the information. We shall rely on the British law system to exercise whatever punishment you feel they deserve for their actions. At least you will be able to see and hear the truth beyond reasonable doubt. The men we would like to interview are Malcolm Friar, Mike Timberson, Jason Nelson, Richard Chance, Stewart Wilson, Peter Jones . . . we know that all these men are at this moment in the UK, and they are available. They should be at the palace door ready to enter by nine o'clock tomorrow morning. If any are dead, we expect to have the body delivered for our verification. There will be no compromise, no exceptions. If those men, every single one of them, are not here by nine o'clock, we will assume you have decided not to save your royal family, their staff and the palace building. Then we will say goodbye and detonate – boom! boom! boom! We shall all fall down. To repeat, people of Britain, we do not intend to kill anybody. Your royal family and staff can be returned alive, and your politicians can be returned alive as well. I will now sign off, and may your God be with you always. I trust that the people concerned will follow our instructions to the letter."

"Stewart, what do you think? Can we trust him? I have a feeling that if we follow his instructions he might just chop our heads off anyway and destroy the palace and everybody in it."

"Well, Prime Minister, I wish he was on our side. He is very clever. He has given us a choice – a very simple choice. We have no way of bargaining. We have no way of compromise. He has backed us into a corner. It is checkmate. If we choose not to appear, we will appear to have no respect for the royal family or even the public. We are deciding their fate, yet we don't actually have any right to. We will probably be charged with treason."

"Stewart, I agree. If he cuts off our heads, he himself will be the loser. He will lose his chance to be seen as a martyr if he goes back on his word. If we save the royal family, we will gain more than we lose by answering his questions. I imagine his questions will be phrased in such a way that we will seem to be the bad guys and he will seem to be the good guy, to give the impression that his religion is true and ours is lies! But what if he is not part of an organisation? What if he is a one-off? All he has said may just be a pack of lies and he is planning to kill everybody? Secretary, can you and the MP chief inspector come in? Chief inspector, I want you to carry out the following: I want you to arrange for every person on this list to be picked up and brought here, in handcuffs or straitjackets if necessary. It has to be every one, walking or carried, no compromise, no excuse. Use as many men as you need. I expect them all here within a couple of hours. We have an urgent agenda to debate. Stewart, I just hope we can get everybody. I am going to spend a few minutes with my family. It'll be just a few minutes. Perhaps you want to do the same."

"Prime Minister, I have sent a car to pick my wife up as I don't want to leave. I might find it difficult to come back if I leave."

An urgent emergency meeting was called at 10 Downing Street by order of the Prime Minister to debate the request of the terrorists who were in control of Buckingham Palace. The lives of the royal family were in danger and the future of England hung in the balance.

"Gentlemen, it's nice to see you all looking so well."

"Prime Minister, cut the crap. You have had us dragged here forcibly and we all know why. I can say simply no – a great big no. No chance. No bloody way."

"Mike, calm down. This is not just crap. We are in a position where we don't actually have a choice. Morally, we cannot murder the royal family in order to save ourselves."

"Murder? Murder, Prime Minister? Where have you dug that up from? Malcolm, Jason, can you believe this fallacy? Don't I – don't we all – have a choice? We have been dragged here under duress. Since when has it become my neck or theirs? For God's sake, come on! Get real! This is serious, not some sort of cock-and-bull story. This is a matter of life or death."

"Mike, the Prime Minister is right. It's not about me or you; it's about the country, about the constitution of the UK. We don't actually count."

"That's very good, Malcolm – really very good. Because of you we have found ourselves jumping in bed and dragged into wars with the Americans. It was just to make *you* look good. As if that wasn't enough, you are now playing at caped crusader, jetting round the Middle East, upsetting God knows who, making millions by the minute, and wanting to start even more wars! I hope you are donating some of the millions to the widows of the dead. You caused their deaths. Now you are blabbing about nuclear weapons. When are you going to wake up, mate? They probably don't actually have nuclear weapons. They don't have stealth bombers waiting to attack us. The only people who have these weapons of mass destruction are the Americans, and now we could lose our lives because of their actions, most of which have been illegal. And never, in fact, despite all the killing and all the suffering, have they secured peace for us at all. No, they bloody haven't! The more roads, Malcolm, you go down, the more graves you dig. I told you not to go down that road, but you never listened. Now look at us walking towards the gallows. Why? I never did anything wrong. I didn't kill that bloke's women and children or torture his friends."

"Look, Mike – we are all probably guilty of waging war in some way or other. If your beliefs were so solid, you could have given up your job at any time; but you were enjoying all the perks, the same as the rest of us. So why the animosity?"

"It's simple, Stewart – very simple, in fact. I would call it old-fashioned common sense. I don't trust that lunatic one little bit, and why should I put my life on the line to save the royal family? They have all had a bloody good life so far. Perhaps it is now time for them to move over to let the people rule the country. We can replace the royal family quite easily, just like Cromwell! But there is no one that I know of to replace me. I have a family who care about me, even if you don't."

"Jason, can we have your thoughts, please?"

"I feel almost the same as Mike, but not exactly the same. If it were just the Queen herself, I know she would agree with Mike. She would not want others to go before her, but – and it's a big but – there are more people involved, a lot more. It is not just the royal family, but all the staff and their families too. This will affect hundreds or thousands of people, and I think that outweighs the risk run by just us few. And let's face it, we can easily be replaced."

"Peter, can you give us your comments, please?"

"I feel a bit isolated. This is all new to me. I have never visited these other countries where Britain has been fighting wars. I wanted to, but I was usually left at home. Nevertheless I do believe we should do the right thing for our country. I am quite prepared to face this man's questions. I'm not sure if I will have the answers he wants, but I can just do my best. I don't feel it is too difficult to trust what he says – after all, he could probably have destroyed the palace and royal family already if he wanted to."

"Thank you, Peter. You really have not missed much, except hours sitting on a plane, hours in the heat and the horrible smells. Believe me, Brighton is better than Camp Bastion. It's not a place where you can have a good night's sleep or even a moment's rest. Thank God I was not there when they suffered that last terrorist attack! The blighters got right inside the base before they were apprehended."

"So Prime Minister, what have you decided? Do we take the high steps to the gallows or the low steps down into hell? What choice do we have, if any?"

"Mike, I know we don't have a majority agreement, but I feel we generally should follow the terrorists' instructions. They will gain nothing by killing us and gain nothing by killing the royal family, but we all have everything to lose if we kill the royal family for him – because that is what it will seem like to the voters for probably the next hundred years. I don't want to be remembered in history for that reason; I don't want my grandchildren being told by the history teacher that their granddad, the Prime Minister, murdered the royal family. I don't want our history to be like the history of some other countries, like Russia, who killed their monarchy many years ago. Our kids deserve better than that. I suggest, gentlemen, that you spend the next hour phoning or writing to your loved ones. I will arrange for the transport."

"Chief Inspector, make sure nobody leaves the building. None of these men, including me, should be allowed to leave. We will need a small bus or similar to take us to the palace. We should leave here at eight a.m., no later, and must have safe uninterrupted passage to the palace, with an escort. Seal any emergency exits on the bus and have a backup bus – no, have two backup buses. We must cover all eventualities. And before we leave, make sure you check, double check, triple check that we are all there. When the bus stops at the palace gate make sure everyone on the bus gets off and follows me across to the entrance. Unless we all enter, the palace could go up in smoke."

"Prime Minister, I will ensure your instructions are carried out to the letter. Good luck, sir. God be with you, and return safely."

"Now, that's a name I have used a great deal lately. Let's hope it's a lucky name for us all?"

"Prime minister, good luck, sir. I really trust you will be back soon."

"I am sure I will, secretary. I am sure we all will be back, and in one piece as well."

CHAPTER FIVE

"Sergeant."

"Commander, the Chief Inspector at Downing Street told me to report to you after I had dropped off the Prime Minister's party at the palace door."

"OK, Sergeant. You need to park up and be ready in case you have a return trip. This constable will show you where to park. Let him know where you will be if not with the bus; he will show you where to get some refreshments."

"Commander, they are all safely in the building now. Did the bus-driver sergeant report to you?"

"Yes, Ken, thanks. Now we must just wait. Keep everybody on their toes and make sure they are all extremely vigilant. Let's hope he keeps his word and is happy with the men he asked for. This lack of communication is diabolical. The only way we will know what is happening is if the palace goes up. We could in an hour's time think all is well, then boom! He never gave us a timescale for when he might release the royal family. I just hope he doesn't go back on his word now he has everybody, and pull the switch."

"Commander, how do you think he will release the royal family? Will he just let them walk out with a crown in one hand and corgis in the other? What do you think?"

"Ken, to be honest, at this moment I don't have a clue. I just hope it's not in a body bag. Hold on – there is some movement in the courtyard. Two cars are coming out slowly. Ken, quick – get out and open the barriers to let them through. Hopefully it will be the royal family."

"All units attention: the two cars leaving the palace are the royal family – I repeat, the royal family. Do not stop them. Do not stop them. Escort both cars with outriders or walkers."

"Commander, I am walking alongside the first car. I can confirm that the two rear passengers are two members of the royal family. They are strapped in with seat belts. Hold on – got it. The driver is not able to open his window or the door. He is wired to a bomb under his seat, so he has to keep the car going."

"OK, Tom. Direct him to Horse Guards Parade. Get the driver to go round in a large circle till we know if it's safe to stop; and clear the area, apart from ambulances, doctors and paramedics."

"Alan, can you make sure the second car follows the first at a reasonable distance? Make sure that if one goes up it doesn't affect the other; and make sure there is no attempt for any reason to open any doors. Assume that both cars are wired the same way."

"Commander Watkins, we urgently – I repeat, urgently – need bomb-disposal teams, and vehicle engineers familiar with Rolls-Royce old models. At times like this you wish the royal cars had number plates for quick and easy identification. Check with Rolls-Royce. Find out where they are serviced. There should be somebody there with a good knowledge. Also check the police-service garages for any engineers with knowledge of these vehicles. Put out a mayday alert. Let's find all the help we can, and have them picked up and taken to Horse Guards Parade. Commander, have there been any further changes at the palace?"

"I have nothing further to report. All is quiet. I've no idea just how long it will be before we get to the next instalment."

At RAF Northolt, South Ruislip, HA4 6NG, Greater London, close to the Second World War Polish war-memorial roundabout on the A40 into London, the SAS operations building is located some distance from the main busy buildings and is out of bounds to all regular personnel. It is complete with its own communications and secure entry system. The necessary operations personnel are flown directly by helicopters from the main base at Hereford. Regular personnel at the RAF base have no actual connection with the goings-on in that building unless a situation arises and they are needed. Should the SAS require transport, the RAF provide the plane and crew, but they are told only the flight plan and have no knowledge of who or what the passengers or cargo might be.

"Evening, Sheppard."

"Viper, good to see you. Glad you were able to make it. Have you been monitoring the developments at the palace?"

"Yes. It's not quite what we have expected or allowed for, so a surprising new chapter opens for us – one we haven't had a rehearsal for."

"Exactly! As you say, it's not what we expected – a complete new page in the book. I have just heard confirmation that members of the royal family have been released, so the door has opened slightly. I want you to go and see what is going on. I have directed Troll and his unit to Heathrow. We have had no word of any terrorist activity there, so he will drop in and trawl the area."

"Sheppard, who has Troll got with him?"

"Viper, Troll has Spider Claw and Poker."

"Sheppard, he should be OK, then. I have Magpie, Eagle and Squirrel."

"Viper, you have dropped Owl from your normal team. Any reason? Any problem?"

"Sheppard, yes. When we got back to Hereford, Owl was hospitalised. That damage he had on his ankle had not healed up. I grabbed Squirrel – he may be short of full combat or overseas experience, but he will be OK. Mind you, it's not that I had a big choice – we are very low in numbers at the moment."

"Viper, when you see Hereford looking like a ghost base, as it is at the moment, it makes you realise just how stretched we are. I just hope the balloon doesn't go up here. It would take a long time to bring some of the regiment back from their overseas operations."

"OK, Sheppard, we are ready to roll. Can you contact the MP at Scotland Yard and ask them if we can have Slingshot down the A40 to the palace, from GPS location 51.5525 0.41722 to GPS location 51.501.364 0.14189?"

"Viper, I will arrange that for you. Good luck. Keep safe out there!"

"Eagle, you drive through the gate. Remember to turn left – your left and my left. Then after 100 yards, at the first roundabout, with the Polish war memorial on your left, go straight across then up and down to the next roundabout, which will be controlled. Pick up the bikers and head straight down the A40, across another roundabout and past Aladdin's Tower on your left. The next junction is Greenford. There is a crossroads with traffic lights then the old Hoover building on your left. Go through the Park Royal underpass under the North Circular and into London area. We should have Slingshot so there will be no need for stopping for traffic."

"Viper, what does this Slingshot actually mean?"

"It's a system the Metropolitan Police brought in, mainly because a lot of VIPs land at Northolt and then use the A40 to get quickly and securely into London. The police have a set of motorbike riders, two up front and two at the rear. If a junction or roundabout is not controlled, the bikers at the front stop the traffic so you go straight through. Then the two behind overtake and takeover the front position, and the other two catch up at the back. They keep swapping from the back to the front: Slingshot."

Major Viper left Northolt base and turned on to the A40 towards London. They were in a black Range Rover lit blue (the high-intensity strobe flashing blue lights on the front, behind the grill, and on the rear of vehicle).

"Major Viper, this is MP. You have Slingshot from second roundabout. Cross traffic held and clear."

"Right, put your foot down, Eagle, and switch to MP frequency. They will keep you updated. Just concentrate on the road in front. You have two or three more roundabouts and an underpass, then clear – just traffic lights for a while."

"Major Viper, you are identified."

"Blimey O'Reilly, Viper, you were right – we now have two up front and two up my backside."

"Eagle, did you think I was kidding you? Others will probably be joining all the time, so we should never lose the ones in front."

"Oh, no, Viper, would I ever think that! Would I ever doubt your words, my leader?"

"Viper, don't you believe anything he says. He usually questions every bloody word he hears. He is not called Eagle Eyes for no reason."

"Don't worry, Magpie – I know him so well. I am fully aware he has eyes instead of ears."

"Squirrel, it won't take you long to measure these two up; take them with a pinch of salt and just throw it over your shoulder – one over the right, one over the left."

"Right, listen up – we are going to Buckingham Palace. No, not to meet the Queen, for a tea party. She's not at home this week. The other royal family members have just been chucked out by a group of unknown targets. Our job is to enter, look and evaluate quietly and invisibly. We need silencers. Load your magazines with low-velocity low-sonic rounds, and remember it is Buckingham Palace. Everything on display will be priceless antiques, so any damage will come out of your wages, probably for the rest of your life. Make sure we don't engage in a firefight; and bear in your mind that if you shoot a corgi thinking it was a lion or a target, you will be thrown in the Tower and probably hanged on a cold and frosty night. Oh, and we won't have darkness, but daylight. The targets will probably be wearing light-coloured robes, which can be very good cover for what's underneath. Eagle and Magpie have seen those before overseas, so, Squirrel, you follow their lead. I will be on point. Make sure your boots are clean – I don't want to get a carpet-cleaning bill. If we take a target out, we must conceal and bag it. I have no information how many or what size or what age. Remember, he might look like a little angelic choirboy, but he could use a AK47 [Russian assault rifle] and cut you in half or blow himself and you up with body explosives. OK, when we get there park up away from the cowboys and tool up. Don't talk to anyone other than hello and goodbye. I will go and get the information update."

"This is Commander Watkins, MP. Major Viper will be joining you in approximately twenty minutes."

"I have received clear instructions. Understood, Commander Watkins. Thank you. MP out."

"Commander, who exactly is this Major Viper – somebody important?"

"Ken, at a guess all I can say is he will be SAS. They use code names and wear uniforms without rank or regiment badges. Ken, don't say a word to anybody and don't expect fireworks. They come and go, and no one knows who they are, so they say, but I have never worked with them. I only know a little from bumping into them at the Yard, as they have an office there in case they are operational in London; but they are totally hush-hush, so that's all I know."

"Commander Watkins, Major Viper."

"Major Viper, I have been expecting you. Glad you are here. I have a copy of the layout of the building for you, but that's all the information I have. I don't know how many persons there are or even where they are located. We have tried to get a thermal-imaging camera – well, we did get one, but we couldn't get it to work."

"That's all right, Commander. I am sure we will manage."

"Oh, by the way, Viper, the royal family are out of the palace at the moment. They are alive, but they are still stuck in their cars as the terrorists have wired them with bombs. We are working out how to defuse them. We are able to converse with the royals, but they can't say for certain how many of the terrorists are in the palace! They have informed us that, in the room they were kept in, there was the one who seemed to be the leader and two others. Others would knock on the door, and one of the men in the room would go and whisper with the door slightly opened, but they never saw who was outside the door. When they were loaded into the cars they think it was the same two men as in the room, but they were all wearing the same robes and they couldn't be sure. They are sorry they can't be more precise. Their main worry was for the safety of the staff and the corgis. They never saw what happened to them and would like to know if they are all right. We promised that as soon as we were aware of their condition we would inform them. In general, the royal family members are very formidable persons. I am hoping these terrorists treated them with total respect – better than the way they treat the women and other people in their own country. Thank goodness none of the royal family decided to be heroes and tackle the terrorists! The family members were all shaken by their experience."

"OK, Commander. I need to speak to you and any others you have direct contact with."

"Right – no problem, Ken. Can you fetch Mike and Phil? Mike, Phil, this is Major Viper."

"OK, we are here to pop in and have a look inside the building to access the problem. We are not here to storm the building – actually, we are not even here. The terrorists are probably tuned in to your radio frequencies, so while we are here you keep them switched off. Now, I notice you have guns everywhere – to me that means cowboys. Yes, I know you are all highly trained marksmen, but that is firing at paper targets. Commander, I know the army jurisdiction is inside the palace grounds, but you would be well advised to have army men deployed next to your men to give you combat experience and support. Let me assure you, if the terrorists decide to leave the building, you would lose seventy-five per cent of your deployed men. You could never visualise just how much lead they would throw at you in a firefight. And you would lose a lot of others too. This unit we are standing in now – an RPG [rocket-propelled grenade] would blow it and the people inside to pieces. I would, at a guess, say that's what happened to the two patrol cars lying burnt out inside the grounds. While on this subject, I will say that we intend to enter and leave by our own method. Now, I want you to go round and tell all your men to keep the safety catch on and their fingers off the trigger, full stop; if we are fired on, we will defend ourselves and fire back and we don't miss. We can't afford to. If you hear gunfire, the noise you hear will be the terrorists, so ensure that you are in a position to respond if necessary. You won't hear our guns. If all is quiet, all is OK. Are you all clear? Any questions? Good, Commander. If you can carry out the requests I have made, I will leave and hopefully return with some good news or at least concise information."

In Horse Guards Parade the two royal cars were being scrutinised so the explosives could be deactivated.

"Ken, the Commander is on the line. He wants to know how we are doing."

"OK, put him on. I will talk to him. Commander, this is Ken. It is slow progress. We have established that the cars don't have to keep moving, but we are not sure about the engines; so we are keeping them running. The Rolls engines can tick over for ever. We have cans with petrol in case we have to top up. Also, ten minutes ago a Rolls engineer arrived from their depot at Park Royal. He was in charge of the last service the cars underwent, so should be a big help. Hold on – I am needed. I will call you back. . . . Commander, we have now worked out the main problem. We think they have wired it so that the door switch that puts the interior light on is probably the trigger. The driver says the terrorists packed a package under his seat, and there are wires coming out of the seat-belt buckle, but we need to tackle the door problem first. The engineer has worked out that we need to cut a hole in the outer body panel to expose the door switch; then we can isolate it and open the door. We can see wires in the rear seat-belt buckles, but they disappear through the gap between the seats. We considered opening the boot to see what's behind the rear seat, but cancelled that idea. The engineer told us there is a light in the boot which comes on when the boot is raised, and when the driver's door opens other lights come on as well, so we need to isolate the driver's door first."

"OK, Ken, take care."

"Commander, update."

"OK, go ahead, Ken."

"Commander – good progress! We cut a hole in the door pillar. I apologise to Rolls-Royce for damaging their bodywork. The engineer told us that although we only cut a four-inch-square hole they will have to replace the complete panel, and it will be a spray job. Apparently Rolls don't just put a patch over and fill it in. Anyway, the engineer is just sorting out the wiring, so hopefully we will be able to open the door. If that works, we will have to do the same on the other doors."

"Ken, are not the interior lights on the same circuit?"

"No, Commander, not on this Rolls-Royce. When the car stops the driver remains seated; his door doesn't open. A footman opens the rear doors to assist the royal family to dismount, exactly the same as if it were a horse-drawn carriage. The driver keeps his foot on the brake to make sure the car (or carriage) doesn't lunge forward and send the royals flying. It's a good system. I am sure the Americans copied that idea for their president, but they haven't worked out that you can have men escorting the car on horseback; they still have men running alongside. Sorry – have to go. I will come back to you."

"Commander, new development. We now have the driver out. He is having treatment so he can move. The poor bloke is not a young man and the ordeal traumatised him completely. He's a total wreck, so we haven't been able to question him yet. The royal family have asked us to look after him. They told us he was locked up somewhere else in the palace and was not with them, so he might be able to give us some useful information. He is very agitated – especially as he is now out and the royal family members are still sitting there. We have given them a mobile phone so they can contact family, etc."

"Ken, can you explain why you have not yet been able to get them out as well.

"Commander, we are not taking any chances – none at all. Although we found out the wiring and bomb under the driver were just an elaborate sham, we can't assume the same about the rear. We don't want to be known for saving the driver and losing the members of the royal family by making that mistake. The royal family members are quite happy with that."

"Ken – good thinking! So what was the sham explosive device all about?"

"Well, Commander, some wiring came from behind the dashboard, but that was just taped up, not connected to anything. The wiring from the seat-belt buckle seemed to be connected to the package under the seat, and we weren't sure if there was another switch which could be triggered if the driver took his weight off the seat. We probed the package a bit, like when you see them taking a tube of cheese out of a block; we then had the powder analysed, and it turned out to be just common washing powder. In the end we got all the powder out, and found it was all washing powder, so we removed all the package and wiring. Then we did a total scan of the driver just in case he was attached to another device. Then we removed him. I would say, Commander, the information I have just given you came as a result of what we did first at the second car. I made a decision off my own bat to tackle the second car first, but I kept that under wraps. I thought if the royal family members knew, they would insist we did the other car first. I also thought you might not agree with my decision, and I knew I would be held responsible if all failed."

"Ken, I appreciate your thinking. We will have a discussion when all this is finished. So you have two drivers out?"

"Yes, Commander, and now we are working on both cars. I have the teams connected, so one leads and the other follows an identical procedure, just as I saw once on a film about two bombs planted on a cruise ship."

"Ken, I remember that film – Richard Harris, if I am not mistaken. Let's hope it works out. I am glad I can't quite remember exactly how the film ended. [In the film one of the bombs did explode, I believe] I will keep my fingers crossed. Keep me informed."

"Commander – good news, the very best. We have the royal party out of both the cars. We have followed your instructions, and we will question them all. We will take them to a safe house. All the family members are extremely annoyed that they could not return to the palace to collect their belongings, and they have asked us to keep them fully informed. They want to be told as soon as we have removed those damn foreign intruders (their own words) and they can safely return. They are very concerned about the staff members, especially as some are old and somewhat frail. The two drivers have been able to tell them that they are all safe and were being well looked after. They said they had been keeping their spirits up by singing songs – Vera Lynn's 'We'll Meet Again', and so on."

"Thanks, Ken. Keep it up and keep us informed about any information you obtain from them. Let's hope we can achieve a similar success at the palace."

"Commander, I am just in time for tea, I hope?"

"Gosh, Viper, I didn't notice you come in! You seemed to be a long time gone. I'm pleased you have returned safely. Are we all clear now?"

"Ah, Captain Lewis, Royal Engineers, great to see you again!"

"Major Viper, very good to meet you again. It's been a long time."

"You know each other?"

"Yes, Commander. I wasn't sure when you said Viper was here that it was the one I know or someone different."

"Really, Captain, just how many Vipers are there in the Army?"

"Well, Commander, I'm not sure, but this is the Viper I know. We go a long way back."

"That's right, Commander. It's good news that Captain Lewis is here. You will need him and his knowledge and experience. The Palace is almost clear, as I will explain in detail."

"Oh, Viper, while you have been busy we have managed to free the royal family safely from their cars. It was all an elaborate hoax – no real explosives or detonators were found, so no real harm has been done apart from the holes we cut in the car bodies."

"That's good news, Commander. It seems as though the terrorists wanted to divert you and gain time. OK now, listen carefully to my briefing and don't interrupt. You can ask questions when I have had my say. Right, you will be pleased to know the terrorists have left the palace, and they have left under their own steam. We had nothing to do with that. They were already gone when we entered. I will explain in a minute. We located the palace staff in this room. They appear to be alive and well. The government members are in the stateroom, here. They are alive. Well, they're all breathing, but not quite with us. They have been drugged and are not coherent. OK, back to the beginning. You would not have noticed the terrorists leaving because they left underground. We found the uncovered entrance to a tunnel in the cellars, about here. I will make more marks on the plans as I go on. Now, Commander, pay attention. You cannot – I repeat, *cannot* – just rush in and free the hostages. That is what terrorists want you to do; and don't think that because the explosives in the royal cars were dummies the same applies to the palace building. They had no intention of killing the royal family, as that would have turned world opinion against them. The sham explosives were arranged to cause confusion and give them plenty of time to get away. You will need to be patient and follow my recommendations to the letter. Now, Captain, you and your squad will have to enter first, and make the place safe and secure. On the map I will mark the traps we found. We did not try to defuse or move any of the items we found, so take great care. There are no devices in the first entrance hall. In this room, here, we located three bodies, all male. Judging by their appearance and weapons, they are probably royal protection officers. There are no blood holes, so I expect they were killed with tranquilliser darts or strangled silently. The main devices are in the main corridors. We didn't find any obvious tripwires as such, but if you look closely you will see where the edges of the carpets have been disturbed. There could be pressure sensors. On both sides of the corridors are tables and statues. That's where we found more devices which are causes for concern. Now, Captain, I have not been long back from AFG [Afghanistan], and there we found an underground laboratory complete with a self-contained workshop. What we discovered in there might have a bearing on these devices. Some of the items were being assembled for suicide bombers and were quite crude, though effective. My main cause for concern were devices which we have established involved biological weapons. Now, looking at the ones the terrorists have installed here, I conclude that they would not have enough explosive to be effective booby traps, unless they are biological. So you won't need your heavy armour-plated suits, and, instead of trying to defuse them, you will need to put them in a sealed container and transport them to a secure lab for them to deal with. Porton Down and Aldermaston are the closest.

The devices we found at the underground lab and examined had been made from normal metal hip flasks, so you can see that they are very light, and easy to carry and conceal. The caps on the flasks had been fitted with the normal primers as used on the case of a standard bullet. The primer is fast-burning, tiny and quite easy to explode. It would blow off the cap without too much noise – a bit like a hammer striking a piece of metal. Then the pressure caused by the primer would cause the biochemical spores stored in the flask to disperse into the air, and you have a simple airborne, undetectable, unnoticeable weapon, deadly to humans. We brought some of the devices back to Hereford for our lab to have a look. They will send copies of their findings to all when ready, but I can say that they reckon one flask could contain enough anthrax spores to disperse over an area of a quarter of a square mile. So you see, Commander, caution is paramount. I would point out that it not likely to be anthrax, but an even more deadly disease, perhaps a locally made, previously unknown type, an upgraded anthrax or even a cocktail combination."

"Viper, sorry to butt in, but I thought this incident was coming to an end. From what you are saying, we are still, more likely, at the beginning. I wasn't expecting this. We are getting well beyond my capabilities and those of my men. I was just expecting to walk in and put matters right."

"Commander, that's exactly how you have to think. It's very easy to rush in to release the hostages thinking you are doing the best for them, etc., etc., but you have to realise they could be the bait to lull you into a false sense of security. You could end up with a vast area contaminated beyond imagination. Anyway, let me continue. It gets worse. Captain, when you clear the corridors your next objective should be the stateroom. You will find the Prime Minister and the others are all sitting in chairs at the table. Their arms and legs are clamped to the chair arms and legs with cable ties. We could not find any booby traps. They all look fast asleep and peaceful. Scattered on the table and the floor are empty and full small bottles and syringes, so be careful where you tread. It's very easy to focus on the persons and not the floor, and it would be easy to break a full bottle with a size-10 boot. I don't know what they were injected with or what's in any of the full bottles. It could be they were injected with something different to what is in the bottles. Captain, your first priority when you enter the room is to clear the floor and table of all the debris. Again place it in sealed containers and transport it away safely. You need then to remove the politicians. That needs to be done properly. I mean, we don't know if they are being used as carriers. Did the terrorists inject them with something contagious? Look at it in another way: why did the terrorists leave them alive? Well, yes, they did say they would, so they must have had a reason, and it could be that they are now carriers. They could spread the disease all over the place. We could have all the Members of Parliament turned into carriers and end up with the entire country covered; so, Commander, you cannot just let them go, even if they wake up and seem OK. My opinion is that they should be removed one at a time, sealed in biological suits or bags and transported to a hospital with isolation units. Then let the medical people look at them. The same applies to the palace staff. Don't just open their door and let them out. They could be infected. And, Commander, the staff need to be checked not just by the medical people, but by security as well. One of them or more could have connections with the terrorists. It's not rocket science. There could be some inside knowledge behind this. We also found a bag filled with mobile phones, which were probably taken from the hostages. On no account just hand them back. Get them to the crime lab for number checking. Check the homes of the hostages. It could be that one is a safe house for our terrorists. I don't think they are so far away. Captain, you need to check that tunnel. Where does it go? We only went twenty-five yards. Some of the floor tiles have been lifted, so there could be a few devices down there as well. There are plenty of ventilation shafts through which a virus could spread from the cellar area into the main building. We need to get hold of a map to see where the tunnel goes. Perhaps some previous monarch had a secret way to one of the local houses so he could visit his mistress, or the tunnel may have access into the Underground train system. Commander, you need to find out if the Underground people have maps showing a connection to the palace. The terrorists must have had previous knowledge of the tunnel – they would not have travelled all the way here on the off chance. There are a great number of immigrants working in the transport and cleaning industries in the UK – one of them could have noticed the plans in one of the offices of the departments who carry out repairs, alterations, etc. There could be hundreds or thousands of moles, sleepers, among the immigrant community. The terrorists were able to leave and enter Buckingham Palace without being noticed, but they may have been filmed by CCTV at the Underground stations. Commander, you need to follow that up. Another thing: in the cellar we found a pile of robes the terrorists have left behind as well as some weapons. I guess they now look like normal businessmen with suits and briefcases. They don't need to have a visible gun. Another use they had for the hip flask was as a sort of a grenade. We found one filled with Semtex, two ounces, so they could use a primer to set off a mighty explosion. Just think – a man dressed in a nice suit and carrying a rolled-up umbrella takes out his hip flask – nothing unusual about that – and boom! He would appear a lot more harmless than some bearded long-haired yobbo carrying a backpack with smoke pouring out as he tries to detonate the home-made chemical bomb he has made with information he copied from the Internet. Right, now we get to the really, really bad news."

"Gosh, Viper, you can't be serious! Don't say you've got something else to cheer us up with? You can't have more – surely not!"

"Oh, yes. Sorry, but I believe this is just the beginning, Commander. We have not yet identified the terrorists' spokesman – in fact, we know nothing about him. We don't know where he came from, how long he has been here, how many others were with him, whether the others were already here before he arrived or even if the one we saw on TV is the main man. He could be just a puppet. Was the main man standing to one side out of sight? Was the main man even here, or is he directing operations from another location, perhaps another country? We don't know. What we do know is that when we find out it will probably be too late. He may have already achieved what he wanted. Has he stopped or is he moving on to his next assignment? We haven't stopped him yet. He may choose to stop, but we don't know how to stop him."

"Oh, my God, Viper! In just a few hours of my life I have begun to feel so inadequate. I feel sick. We really don't have a clue. This is not just cops and robbers, like what we are used to dealing with. This is way outside the bounds of our knowledge and experience, despite all the meetings we have had about how to deal with terrorists. The few occasions we have had bombers in reality were like schoolboy pranks compared with this. I am going to have to take this up with my superiors. It's way outside my capabilities. Captain, we will need a lot more assistance from the army. I feel we need to go back to looking after robbers and traffic and hand the whole thing over."

"Commander, the army units which are qualified to handle this situation are not in the UK at the moment. They are tackling similar problems in another part of the world. My unit is all there is. Another week and we would have been deployed overseas as well. You can now see why we, the army, oppose the government's cutbacks. We don't need fewer trained men; we need more highly trained technicians – men who think with their brains and not their rifles. It's become a question of capability, not just manpower. How many guns have we deployed in this situation? yet we have not had to use one. Not one shot has been fired. We have a crisis, and from what Viper has said we could end up with thousands dead, and the terrorists have achieved that without firing a shot or creating an explosion, apart from the two patrol cars. I think you would agree, it makes us seem a bit silly having so many persons walking around displaying weapons."

"Gentlemen, we need to focus on the situation we have at this moment. Let me explain the main problem here. Now, I explained about the laboratory workshop we came across, but I didn't tell you (because I wasn't sure it would be relevant) that we found another device on the roof of Buckingham Palace. It was larger than a hip flask, and this device could be an urban nightmare. It could wipe out a million people, not with explosives but totally silently. I believe that this is the main reason behind this terrorist

71

activity. I believe the royal family and the government business has been a red herring to distracted us from the real reason. I am convinced that the terrorist agenda is to create a situation similar to but greater than the bubonic plague of yesteryear. It is simpler than radiation from a nuclear device. This simple device built using relatively inexpensive ingredients could prove more deadly than setting off a few bombs; 9/11 would seem trivial in comparison. Compared with the few thousand deaths the 9/11 terrorists caused, you could have 6 million people slowly dying. London could become a graveyard. I am sure you will have seen similar happenings in disaster movies on the television, usually American-made. They are probably watched by the world's terrorists too, and they will have given them plenty of ideas to put into practice."

"Viper, you need to explain this device. Why has it caused you to think like that? Can't we disarm it?"

"Captain, this device is simple to build. You can go round the local stores and buy the items and nobody would think you need to be followed and monitored. There are no chemicals or bags of fertiliser because it's not explosive. Let me draw a sketch. We have a metal container, say three litres, with a round neck. We fit two non-return valves from the local plumbing shop to the sides of the container. We buy from the car shop a small compressor – the sort to blow your tyres up. Some new cars have one in their boot instead of a spare wheel. We need a computer laptop battery, and from the electronics store we buy a timer as used on TV appliances for recording films and other programmes – the type with several day or week settings. We need a thin metal or hard plastic dome-shaped disc which we can push in the vessel neck to seal it. We mount the whole thing in a box. We connect a small length of tubing from the compressor to one of the non-return valves, and connect the compressor through the timer to the battery, which we need to have fully charged. Using a suitable syringe we pump the biochemical mixture through the other non-return valve and fill the container with our lethal toxic mixture. Now, the timer triggers the compressor, which pumps air into the vessel; the pressure builds up and the sealing disc pops out, blowing the chemicals and viruses out into the atmosphere. The biological idea is nothing new. Saddam in Iraq used similar methods against the Kurdish people, and I believe that was just an experiment. He used the Kurdish people as unaware guinea pigs. I don't recall the Americans saying they had found and neutralised all the biochemical weapons in Iraq. We do know they were working on a camel-pox virus, and that has been classified as one of the deadliest animal pathogens. There might be plenty of barrels of the stuff still out there somewhere. And bear in mind that at this very moment, all over the world, there are persons using their knowledge and brainpower to design and make deadly devices using everyday items. Who knows exactly what they might come up with? You can't produce an antidote till you know what you need it for, and by then it's probably too late anyway."

"Viper, as you say, it's very simple, very cheap, but – bloody hell! – very effective. There's no loud bang, so nobody runs away, no screaming people. They just stay around, breathing in the toxic air. Even then they might not react for hours or days, and by then the terrorists will have long gone to safety to sit back and enjoy the devastation."

"That's right, Captain. Now, the one up on the roof has had some extras fitted. It has a lid over the box. Don't touch! I had a look inside through a ventilation hole with my little 'snake scope'. The box has a pendulum switch connected to the compressor, so if you move the box or lift the lid you will start the compressor. I could just read the timer setting as five days, but couldn't see how long is left. My idea is to get one of those robot surgical appliances they use in keyhole surgery and clamp the tubing from the compressor just as they clamp a vein to stop the blood flow, a bit like cutting the umbilical cord. Then we can pull or cut the tubing off the compressor, and it won't matter if it starts. Just in case, we could cut the battery wires. It should then be safe to lift the lid (we'll need to make sure we seal the neck and disc securely) then lift the vessel, place it in an airtight container and send it away to the lab."

"Viper, that sounds too easy – are you sure, 100 per cent?"

"Captain, the terrorist probably does not know we have found the workshop and already have one of the devices at Hereford.

If they realise we have been able to disarm the device, they will come up with a mark-2 version with more gismos. There are quite a lot more sensors, etc., they could incorporate. Oh, one more thing, Captain: don't just cut the wires to the compressor. They might not be the same, but on the one we have they have used multiple fine-wire cable. If you cut the wire, your cutter will make the connection between the wires and start the compressor; so do the tubing method first. Oh, Commander, for the finale you will need to think about possible evacuation – not just of the local area, but of the entire population of London. You will need to get the boffins involved."

"Viper, that would be a total impossibility. You can't just uproot 6 million persons, including thousands of persons at present in hospitals and businesses. Where would you put them all?"

"Commander, you will need the government to implement any contingency plans they have drawn up for important persons, if any. We have wasted time and effort searching for terrorists with guns and bombs, and we have built up our security to prevent hijacking, but we have totally missed the really simple way to remove the Western dominance of the world without firing a single shot or making a single explosive device. How come we have spent so much time and wasted so many lives looking for weapons of mass destruction, which we were misled into believing were in existence, when weapons of mass destruction can be carried on a single person's body or briefcase. One suicide bomber blows himself up and kills and injures a few others, but imagine one person with a pocket full of a deadly biochemical cocktail on a train or in a crowded shop, just walking around spreading a plague without having to blow himself up. Wholesale panic and fear will be the inevitable result."

"OK, Viper, I hope we can stop that device before the time is up. How long do you think we have?"

"Captain, I think we must have a couple of days at least. I think the terrorists, despite their claim not to be worried about dying, will want to get back home to claim victory. Let me know how you get on. Here – have one of our radios. I will tell Sheppard your frequency so he can contact you direct, in case the lab at

Hereford comes up with any more information. And if you relay your method and details to Sheppard, he will pass them on to any others if required elsewhere."

"Viper, it's nice to know that I am being the guinea pig."

"Captain, you know I wouldn't leave you to it if I didn't believe you could do it. There is not much more I can do here, so I will return to base. I've a feeling we will have more to come. You know as well as I do that these so-called goatherds have an amazingly cunning intellect. They might not fire their guns in a perfectly straight line, but they know that if they fire thirty rounds in the general direction they will probably score a hit. They also know how to conceal themselves, and they know the different ways to kill. They enjoy killing people and they don't have any qualms about killing women and children."

"Commander, we are leaving now, back to base. Keep Sheppard informed of your progress. If you locate the terrorists, take care and inform us and we can respond."

"Thanks, Viper. It has been nice meeting and working with you."

CHAPTER SIX

"Sheppard, this is Viper. We are about to leave BPAL [Buckingham Palace] and return to base."

"Viper, Sheppard. Can you hold your present position? Confirm?"

"Sheppard, Viper. Holding. Do you have a reason? Details, please?"

"Viper, Troll has broken down [compromised] location. LHR [Heathrow] needs assistance. Can you proceed to his GPS location? The call is amber [urgent – requires firearms and medical help]."

"Sheppard, Viper. Able to respond. Mobile on way."

"MP, this is Major Viper. We are mobile. Need Slingshot to Heathrow maintenance area, GPS location 51.47238, 0.45094. Can you assist? Eagle, you take over drive."

"Viper, MP. Slingshot in operation. Can you proceed to end of Mall?"

"MP, Viper. Many thanks. We are in a black Range Rover, light blue. Can you identify. Eagle, switch to MP frequency. He will give you specific instructions."

"Troll, Viper. En route. ETA, forty-five minutes. Your situation, please?"

"Viper, Troll. Good to hear your voice. We have broken down [compromised]. Man down. Not able to move or relocate. We have located targets, brown ball. They have second level in front of our location. We are blue ball; they are T1 yellow and T2 green and have full spread [cover] of middle pocket. You will need to use pink ball lid [building roof] for high ground. Distance 100 narrow clicks [range 100 metres]. Hope you have brought Long Henry."

"Troll, Viper. Understood. Long Henry available. ETA, thirty minutes."

"Viper, Squirrel. Who exactly is this Long Henry chap when he's at home?"

"Squirrel, some time back I was over in the States with the navy Seals and they showed me their latest toy, a Barrett 50-calibre sniper rifle. It's semi-automatic so you can get several rounds off in quick succession. It is also heavy and over five foot long, so has a tripod, and it recoils like a horse's kick in the teeth. The Seals had definite confirmed kills at 1,800 metres in Iraq. It also has a thermal-imaging sight so you can see the target on the other side of a brick wall. The 50-calibre round will pass through a brick wall, through the target and out through another wall on the other side. It's not much use for close-up or street fighting. They gave me one as a present to bring home, told me it was called the Long Henry. I think it was named after some cowboy's Winchester or Springfield buffalo rifle of yesteryear. I've kept it in case it is needed. It looks as though it can earn its keep. Squirrel, just so you know the information Troll was giving us, we use the snooker table layout as a guide when we are describing the battlefield. From what he said, he is pinned down in open space and the targets have control of the field of fire to his front, left, right, and flank. To release him he wants me to take to the roof of the building at his rear, so I am above and can shoot down at the targets while they are distracted, looking downwards. Sheppard, Viper. I have voice contact with Troll. Do you have any further information?"

"Viper, Sheppard. Troll was trawling [searching for insurgents] LHR and was surprised by invisible [concealed/hidden/unknown] targets using smoky RPG. Spider is down. Both walkers [legs] damaged, so parallel lift [stretcher] is required."

"Sheppard, Viper. Are Troll's new friends lonely [any other terrorists]?"

"Viper, Sheppard. Confirm: friends are lonely. Confirmation that LHR is saturated [large number of visible normal persons]; quantity of targets [known terrorists] unknown at present. No other corking [gunfire] reported."

"There's Troll's vehicle. Park up. OK, tool up. Use flash covers, not silencers, and high-velocity magazines while I have a look. OK, Troll is fifty metres in front of this building. There is no back-door cover, so, Magpie, you take left pocket. Eagle, right pocket. Squirrel and myself will take the roof. Troll told me targets 1 and 2 are on the second floor and have end-window access. Both have HMG [heavy machine gun] and RPG. I want to take out both. Will take left first, yellow. When I am ready, Magpie, I will want you to give a couple of three burst at the targets to draw their attention, then pull back in case they send a smoky [rocket] your way. Then we do the same to the right side, green. OK, Eagle? Right, let's go hunting. Troll, Magpie, Eagle, Viper. We will take our yellow first. Two targets. HMG manned; RPG not visible. Magpie, three count then your burst. Three, two, one."

Bang! bang! bang! **Bang! Bang!**

"Two targets down. Eagle, green, three count."

Bang! bang! bang! **Bang! Bang!**

"Two targets down. Magpie, Eagle, cover forward area. Troll, come home to pink. Squirrel, cover blue centre area. I want to keep an eye on target's brown location. Viper, Magpie and Troll in nest; Spider in web. Area secure and maintained and locked [area covered]. Squirrel, make your way down to vehicles. I'll join you in a minute."

"Sheppard, Viper. We have major compromise [difficult situation unable to resolve safely]. We are returning to base. ETA, forty-five minutes."

"Viper, Sheppard. Give details."

"Sheppard, Viper. Believe targets have installed a shower system [biochemical device], GPS location 51.47238, 0.45094."

"Viper, Sheppard. Confirm details."

"Sheppard, Viper. Believe type of shower set up identical to the one installed at BPAL. We need to evaluate."

Viper and Troll units return to operational office at RAF Northolt.

"OK, good result, you three. When you two opened up the HMG target swung towards you but didn't spray immediately as they were setting up the RPG; so I was able to take them both before they fired a shot. So well done. OK, help Troll and the others. They have quite a few dents [wounds requiring medical attention]. And make sure Spider gets to the medical unit. Clean tools, stow, and get food, but keep ready in case we have a quick shout [emergency situation to attend]. I will be with Sheppard."

"Viper, how sure are you about the shower at LHR?"

"Sheppard, not 100 per cent. I did not go and see as we didn't have any biochemical protective suits. After we removed the four targets I kept scanning and found another three on the roof, but they were paper [not armed]. I kept on scanning and they left the roof. They went to where the eliminated metal [armed] targets were and had a good look around. Then they left, taking nothing with them. I did not engage in case I couldn't eliminate them all, and might have caused one to switch on the shower. Then I went back, scanning where they had been on the roof, and spotted the device. It looked very similar to the one we found at BPAL so it is probably the same set-up. I assume the fires at LHR are a sort of diversion while they planted the shower. Troll told me they trawled LHR and found no targets or obvious evidence of terrorist activity. The damage appears to be accidental, but it is extensive. They were caught by surprise when they arrived at the abandoned isolated maintenance terminal area."

"Oh, Viper, Captain Lewis told me to inform you they were able, following your advice, to deactivate the devices at BPAL. The timer was on a seven-day setting and the five days you observed was the time left. The Commander is pleased he doesn't have to evacuate London, as you feared he might. They have also located the missing army rapid-response unit and the gatehouse officers in the back of a UPS van, all deceased.

There is no visual cause of death. Five bodies were retrieved from CO19 cars – the result of an RPG or landmine. All the bodies at BPAL have been bagged and isolated for examination."

"Sheppard, that time factor – well, that's a big worry."

"Viper, why do you think?"

"Sheppard, I had been thinking about the setting-up procedure the targets might have used. We have not been able to establish if the two target units we have dealt with so far are the only two, or whether BPAL was the first objective and LHR the second; or was LHR the first and BPAL the second? The fact that the BPAL setting had five days to run makes me think BPAL was the first; but if the LHR device has a longer time to run, perhaps that was the first. Either way, the long time settings might be for totally different reasons. Either the time settings were to allow the targets to get away or to allow time for the setting-up of more shower units at other locations. We need to establish if the targets have left the country, and that should be our number-one priority."

"Sheppard, you will need to send the cleaners in to remove those four targets at LHR, but not before Captain Harris has deactivated them and removed the shower device, and the building is cleared. Tell him to tackle that urgently and to inform us of the time setting. Let's hope we have a similar long time frame. Suggest he gets up to the roof from the outside, as I have not done a reconnaissance inside the building for any other devices. It will probably be the same set-up as at BPAL. It might also be an idea, after he has finished, to invite him to attend our unit at Hereford and debrief. He should have some good useful experience to pass on."

"Viper, I have just had a video copy arrive by courier. Apparently they found it at BPAL. They think the terrorists left it behind. The MP commander wants us to have a look."

"That looks like the same man as before. Perhaps he wants to be an actor. I will put the sound on."

"Hello, people of Britain. Your capital city, London, has been violated and is burning for you to see what can happen when you illegally attack, invade, steal a country which is not yours

*and never can be. I want to explain to you just how useless
the men you vote for really are. You will know by now that we
have made them look like idiots. Let me also tell you just how
good your MI5 and MI6 security services are – the services
which are supposed to keep you safe in your beds. Let them
explain to you just how we were able to walk into Buckingham
Palace and capture your royal family; had we chosen to, we
could have destroyed your royal family and reduced the palace
to rubble. Let them explain how we took over and destroyed
your main airport, and brought total havoc to worldwide air
travel. We could have eliminated your government, and we
might have destroyed your country, but when we found it rather
boring we just left and went home. If you travel the world
killing and destroying innocent people and their countries
you will be eliminated along with the other superpower
warlords. You have a choice. Don't forget to thank the
Americans for causing our visit, and remember how well they
protected you in your hour of need."*

"Sheppard, that video has been doctored, put together. Look –
in the background. The window – see? The curtains have not
been drawn properly. There's a little gap. If you blow that up, you
may be able to identify where it was filmed. I believe the location
video was done before the person video. He was added later.
They probably had several location videos made by persons who
did not know what they were for, so the location on this one might
not be the one where the shower device is located. We could
waste our time and effort, but we can't afford to ignore this possible
clue."

"Viper, I can see that. But what are you getting at?"

"Well, the video is a plant. They know we will be able to identify
the location of the room where the video was made, because
they have set it up so we can. When we identify the location, we
are meant to go rushing round, burst in and pat ourselves on the
back, not realising we have turned the shower on. Sheppard, you
need to tell the security services that if they locate the room they
mustn't enter. Tell them to check the roof first, then speak to
Captain Lewis. He can tell them what to look for and what not to

do. If that location is in London, as I expect, the Commander may have to evacuate the city. We need total cooperation between all departments and services. If they have been able to walk in, as they say, we could have shower devices all over the city. In the video he said he was capable of reducing the country to rubble. Our security services will interpret that in their silly way and be looking for bombs, because that's all they know about, but just think how big a bomb would be needed to carry out his threat. It would have to be nuclear, and then the country would be uninhabitable for 1,000 years. A small biochemical device would wipe out the people without using a single bullet or bomb, and the terrorists needn't lose a single man. Then they could use the country for their own people. After all, it is no use wiping out a country that could otherwise produce food for your own survival. We have to believe him – he has not told a lie as yet. I feel he wouldn't say anything unless he means what he says. It doesn't matter if we don't understand, as long as he achieves his goal."

"Viper, I know you are not always right, but also that you are rarely wrong."

"Sheppard, look – we have had two groups of targets. Were they totally independent of each other? I don't think so. I believe they were one unit that split up, so I would guess they entered the country together or filtered in individually and met up, but how did their weapons enter the country? Did they come in one way and their material come another?"

"Viper, which way are you thinking?"

"I think they came in as a complete unit, then split up. The easiest way would have been in a container by sea. I spent some time at a container port on the east coast, and I saw how easy it would be to smuggle a small army in. The contents of some of those containers are loaded on lorries and carried out of the port without being properly checked. If the containers are from, say, Holland and contain perishable produce they travel straight through. The only check I saw was the temperature gauge, and that seemed to be in order to make sure the produce was OK. It would be quite easy to lock the temperature gauge at the right reading. Then having hot bodies in the container wouldn't show. There are so many containers that they can't X-ray them all. The only ones that are sure to be X-rayed are the ones from dodgy countries. Details of all the containers are entered on a computer system – a very good system – but it would be possible for the computer operator to be a mole. I watched one from India. He seemed very competent in his job, but he could quite easily have arranged for a container to be taken off a ship and placed in a special area to be picked up quickly, and so on. I wouldn't mind betting that no security checks are made on the manpower at the docks. As I watched the Indian computer operator I wondered if he had any family. It would be easy for the terrorists to threaten his family if he didn't cooperate. So did our targets arrive in one container and then disperse? MI5 will need to trawl all the container ports, ignore the containers that have come a long way and check the ones that have come a short way – especially the ones which are said to contain perishable goods, as they would pass through the ports quickly. They need to look for the improbable and not the probable."

"Viper, I will pass on your recommendations. I am glad you are on our side and not a terrorist."

"I don't find it difficult to think like them. The persons I have met from MI5 and the CIA have trouble finding terrorists because they don't and can't think like them. A normal Englishman or American hasn't lived and grown up with the people who become terrorists, so can't think or act like them. There is a saying, set a thief to catch a thief, but we don't have our very own terrorists to help us through this crisis."

"Sheppard, I have been looking at the map. The targets at BPAL and LHR must have an escape route, but it would be more or less impossible to travel overland. On the map, here and here, there is total congestion, so I think they must be using the Underground train system. That would be an ideal way for them to leave London. It would be very easy for them to melt in with the normal passengers. Just wearing a suit and carrying a small briefcase or umbrella, they wouldn't seem a threat to anybody. I have checked with MP, and the Underground system is all working apart from LHR express (the Heathrow section). That's been shut down. At first I thought the targets from LHR might use the LGW [Gatwick] connection, but that is shut down as well. Then again, LGW is full and there are not many planes taking off, so I've discounted that. All other trains are running normally, so now the London targets could have caught the train and travelled to this area, here. They could have met up with the LHR targets round about this area, here and here."

"Viper, do you think they will be all heading for the coast?"

"Possibly, but not for a normal boat connection. It would be good sense to have ports and marinas checked by local police, but I have come up with this theory. The Channel is very busy, but it is difficult to stop and search or track every boat. A boat comes up the Channel, and on board are two or more seaplanes. They take off and fly low, below the radar, over the coast and land at a lake or reservoir in this area, here. The ship carries on, perhaps to Dover or Belgium, then turns round and travels back the way it came, looking totally innocent. The targets meet up with planes, take off, and land close to the ship, and the targets are away. They would not even have to load the planes – they could sink them; so if the ship was stopped, there'd be no incriminating cargo and nothing to connect anyone on board with terrorist activity."

"Viper, as I said, I am glad you are on our side and not theirs."

"Sheppard, you need to contact the coastguard. See if they have noticed any planes flying around in the last few days. I will look at more detailed maps to try to identify possible water landing areas round this part of the coast. And we shouldn't forget the tunnel – that would be an easy alternative way of getting home again. There's a good rail link from London or Dover. We are probably looking for a group of ten to fifteen men, all wearing normal suits. They might be travelling together, singly or in pairs. They might even have women with them, or even men dressed as women, wearing the burka or similar, and some of them could actually be teenagers. It would make sense if they travelled as a large mixed party rather than a few men on their own. We need to focus on normal-looking people – anyone who seems unlikely to be a terrorist. They are more likely the ones that are. We don't need to waste time picking up persons who have been under surveillance, because this group will have had no contact with any of those persons, and they don't communicate using the Internet or phone system. We can be sure about that because otherwise they would have been detected before now. I think we could list them as the ghost squad."

"Viper, Sheppard. Coastguard reported that two or three small planes crossed the coast three days ago, but they didn't seem to be together. They did not fly in a group."

"Sheppard, Viper. See if you can obtain pictures of the types of small seaplanes they use up in Canada. Last time I was there I travelled about on one. They use them like cars and taxis as there are no roads, only rivers and lakes. Send the pictures to the coastguards and see if they can identify the ones they have seen?"

"Viper, Sheppard. Yes, the coastguards have recognised the seaplanes by the floats underneath."

"Sheppard, that's good. Now we need to locate where they landed. I am sure it must be on water as they have no landing wheels."

"Viper, Sheppard. Coastguards have just reported similar seaplanes passing over the coast and heading out to sea. They were too far away from the coastguard location to be identified with certainty. I have asked the coastguard to let me know what ships are in that area. Alert navy patrols in that area, and ask them to intercept and search any ships."

"Viper, Sheppard. Bad news. The coastguard and navy report heavy seas. It is not possible for planes to land. They will continue to monitor shipping in the probable area, but the planes were flying low and they have disappeared. The navy has put a helicopter up to have a look round, but conditions are poor. You never know, one of the planes might have tried to land or could have ditched."

"Sheppard, Viper. Blast! Lady Luck doesn't seem to be on our side. OK, try plan B. If they can't land in the Channel, they must go to France. There is plenty of space and water round Brest. Notify the French secret service and get them to look. It will be difficult for them because there are quite a few British businessmen who live in that area and work in the UK. They have their own planes and landing sites. The chance of the targets being spotted is not good, unless they land on somebody's fishing area. Then there would be an uproar. They might head for Santander to meet with a ship, or they could try Portugal – somewhere with good road or rail links. From my information I believe there are three possible areas where those planes might have landed in the UK. They could have used any of them, or all three. All of them are located in the Sussex area. Weirwood Reservoir is approximately two miles long; Ardingly Reservoir is three miles long, and Bewl Reservoir has a perimeter of twelve-plus miles or more. All have wooded areas, so a seaplane could be concealed from the air. Bewl would be my choice. It covers a large area and is surrounded by woodland and farmland and fairly isolated. It does have sailing club, fishing club and other water-sports clubs, but even so there shouldn't be too many people around at this time of year. Contact the local police and ask them to drop in and have a look. I know the birds have flown, but they may have left something useful behind. Tell them they need to be vigilant and not to pick anything up, no matter how innocent-looking."

"Viper, Sheppard. I have some feedback from the reservoir enquiries. It looks like you were right. It almost certainly was Bewl. The local police found two abandoned taxis. They were missing from Uckfield Station and were found in a lane next to Bewl Reservoir. They had been noticed by local walkers, but it was assumed that the occupants were out walking. However, the police found the drivers' bodies dead in the cars' boots. Again there was no obvious cause for the deaths. Two anglers were also found deceased – again no obvious cause. The four bodies have been 'bio-bagged' and will be delivered and isolated for examination. Walkers were questioned, but reported no unusual happenings."

"Sheppard, Viper. It looks as though they used the Oxted–Uckfield rail line. They could have picked that up at Clapham Junction, London bridge or elsewhere and travelled to the end of the line, Uckfield Station. If they took taxis, why only two? Why three planes? I would like to know if there were just three in each taxi. Perhaps someone at the station noticed. Each plane had room for only two passengers each, that equals six; but we know three left LHR and there were nine robes left at BPAL, which suggests that there were at least twelve targets. If only six went out by planes, where are the other six-plus? Are they still here, or did they leave another way, like through the Channel Tunnel? I wonder. And did the planes only have the pilots, or did they bring in some more targets? They could have quite easily brought a few more in. If so, are they to carry out further atrocities? It would be good tactics to take out one unit and drop another unit in behind us while we spend all our time looking for the first lot. The second unit could be long-term sleepers, to hide until needed. I expect the ones who left by plane were the important ones, and the others are more likely foot soldiers; but, then again, it is always dangerous to assume. Some of the first unit could be sleepers too, gone to ground somewhere in this country."

"Viper, Sheppard. I can hear the wheels grinding away from here. It is quite painful, knowing you could be and probably are right."

"Sheppard, Viper. It has always bothered me, the way the operation flowed. OK, it might be down to forward planning. They might have spent years gathering information and putting it all together. I don't believe it was all down to some goatherd sitting in a cave in the mountains. We do the same, but we usually go to the site and dig in before we execute; and if there is a problem, we abort. You can't tell me they left their cave, travelled across the world, turned up in this country, carried out their plan and left totally without detection. They must have had a base here or in Europe. I believe the plan was hatched on our doorstep, then when ready they ordered in the cavalry to execute. We have followed the Americans and moved our operations to terrorist locations on the other side of the world, but we have left our back door open. How many potential terrorists have we invited into this country with our immigration schemes? And what of the rest of Europe? OK, we have noticed a few, and we have caught them, but that is because they were obvious for some reason. But how many more are out there? I'm not referring to immigrants who go round denouncing us and our beliefs, but the ones who are real thinking terrorists. They appear to be normal, honest and law-abiding. They don't walk around carrying AK47s or shouting the odds. Perhaps some who were at BPAL are now back at their homes in the UK, ready to melt back into their everyday lives and jobs and waiting for their next instructions."

"Viper, Sheppard. Update from the reservoir police units: there were only two taxis available at the train station at that time. The drivers were not reported as missing because they usually spent a lot of time in the pub while waiting for the next train to arrive. They were not immediately missed by their families. At the reservoir police found some witnesses to the three seaplanes taking off in the middle of the lake, but because light was fading they noticed no markings. They assumed they were to do with some film being made or something to do with the environment. There was nothing to give them cause for alarm. No one could tell us how long the planes had been there. The police are leaving some officers in the area to question any other members of the public who turn up for fishing or walking. The fishermen found dead at the scene were both loners, so they were not missed by anyone. I expect they were simply in the wrong place at the wrong time. The police are searching the area, but I don't think they will find anything."

"You know, Sheppard, some time back, while out and about, I came across some men in a dead-end road. They seemed quite normal – nothing suspicious. They were from the water board and they explained to me that they were flushing the main owing to some repair work down the road. They fitted a standpipe to a connection on the main, then opened the tap and let the water rush out to check it was clean. Apparently this is the normal procedure. They told me there were hundreds of thousands of these standpipe connections on the water network. Now, at that time there had been an outbreak of legionnaires' disease which had been traced to the water in cooling towers. The bacteria thrive in water. It occurred to me that if terrorists wanted to cause the maximum damage, say to a town or city, they could quite easily do so by adding a fatal disease – a virus or strain of bacteria – into the drinking-water system. Think how many times you have noticed a small van at the side of the road with the name of the local water board on the side. I bet you take no notice of what is going on. They may carry an ID card, but most people can't tell whether it is genuine or not. On one of our training exercises we had to merge with different police forces, and we were able to do so at every single one without being detected or even challenged."

"Viper, Sheppard. I follow your reasoning, but how would terrorists be able to contaminate the water supply?"

"Sheppard, Viper. This is my theory: they would use a small gas bottle – the large gas bottles would be too heavy and clumsy to use, so the ones they use in the medical departments at hospitals or on ambulances, quite small and easy for one person to carry, would be best. The terrorists would fill them with a culture of the disease, and pressurise the contents. Then they would connect it to a standpipe anywhere on the water mains, and open the valve on the bottle and the tap on the standpipe. The bottle contents would be forced into the water mains because the pressure in the bottle is higher than the mains water pressure (which I think is only about fifteen psi, so they would only need, say, fifty psi in the bottle). They have now added a waterborne virus or bacterium to the mains drinking-water system. How would anybody ever know how it was done? They would probably never imagine it was done deliberately. They might blame some farmer's slurry leakage or similar. It would be extremely difficult to pinpoint the source, and the terrorists would disappear without trace. They could easily carry this out all over the country, and every time a tap is turned on for drinking, washing, filling a cistern, flushing a loo, filling a bucket or washing a car the disease would spread. Not only that, but when people are admitted to hospital they could be inadvertently given contaminated water to drink. We would have to live on bottled water, except that bottled water would be just as easy to contaminate. This very simple idea would be very simple to implement and very difficult to counteract."

"Viper, Sheppard. I will say it again: you should be leading a think tank of scientists and engineers instead of out in the field stalking already established known targets."

CHAPTER SEVEN

Back at Downing Street somebody was needed to lead the country in the Prime Minister's absence.

"Minister, somebody needs to take charge. You are the most senior of your party and, technically, would have been the Deputy Prime Minister if there was no coalition. I feel you should take the responsibility while the Prime Minister is unavailable."

"Are you totally sure about this, secretary?"

"Yes, we have no other choice. The Prime Minister and Deputy Prime Minister are out of action – the others too. We don't know how long they will be unavailable, so we have no choice. We can't just shut up shop till they return. What are the legal procedures for a situation of this kind? It's never happened before, so we are in uncharted territory, to say the least. One thing is certain: if we don't act quickly, we could have some general using the army to take over the country."

"Oh, really, secretary? I don't think so, do you?"

"Minister, it is happening almost on a daily basis out there in the world, so why not here? And, minister, don't forget the Americans. They have land bases in this country and navy warships anchored at and off Portsmouth at this very minute. There was a Cabinet debate about that in the last few days. The country is basically run by the civil servants, so the everyday running is not a problem in the short term, but at this moment we don't have a Prime Minister in office. In the normal way this is not a problem as the Deputy Prime Minister would step up and all the protocols would be in place. However, because the Deputy Prime Minister is also unavailable we have to look at a different strategy. We need to produce a person to be the Acting Prime Minister, and the Liberal Party need to produce a person to be the Acting Deputy Prime Minister. Likewise, all the missing ministers will have to be replaced by temporary ministers. The Labour Party does not have the same problem, but they cannot take over the government, and under the present circumstances they could not push for a general election. The coalition has to remain in control and has to appear to *be* in control. I have spoken to the medical consultants, but they are unable to identify the drugs our colleagues were injected with, and cannot say how long they might be out of action or even *if* the ministers will recover."

"Secretary, I can see your difficulty. I will arrange a meeting of the other available Cabinet members of my party and discuss the problem. I would appreciate if you will attend and assist with the protocol to ensure a correct and acceptable outcome. Regarding the Liberal Party, they will have to arrange a meeting of their own."

"I would also point out, minister, that whoever is selected as Acting Prime Minister can't just move into Number 10, as the existing Prime Minister's family are in still in residence. The Prime Minister himself could return at any moment, so we can't expect his family to move out. Any moving-out would have to be a decision taken by the Prime Minister's wife and family."

"Secretary, I can assure you that the correct protocol will be followed to the letter. I believe in my heart that the Prime Minister will be back and in control before too long."

An emergency meeting was called. In attendance were the Acting Prime Minister, the Acting Deputy Prime Minister, and all available Cabinet ministers and temporary Cabinet members of the coalition parties.

"Gentlemen, I would like to open the meeting with a minute's silence in remembrance of the persons who have lost their lives, the ones who at this moment are losing theirs and the ones fighting to keep theirs in the UK and the world. . . . Thank you. As you all are aware, we have been ravished by unforeseeable events that have taken place in the last five days. I cannot even try to recount the full details, as I don't know them. I am aware that none of you do either – we are still reaching out and clutching at straws. When I saw the first television pictures of some of the devastation, I thought, 'This can't be real!' It seemed like a movie. I was not prepared for what I saw when I visited Heathrow myself. I saw the horrific and vast carnage at first hand. I was so moved. I did not ask the media not to broadcast the pictures of myself being sick; most of them were being sick too. The stench! The heaps of burning flesh! The bodies sitting upright in rows – persons who had been firebombed and cremated while still sitting in their seats! The sight was far too overpowering for my body's defences. I was in a state of total horror. I will have nightmares for the rest of my life. For the first time in my life I was witnessing a disaster where the dead vastly outnumbered the living. The area was littered with the burnt-out shells of vehicles. I am glad that the Prime Minister has not had to see what we have witnessed, and I wish him and the other ministers a speedy recovery. Now, gentlemen, we have to sort out this mess and put the country back on its feet. The television pictures cannot convey the full horror of what happened. I don't personally know the solution to this crisis. I feel we have to pull together and pool resources, knowledge, information ideas. Any suggestions? Defence Minister, can you start? Give us what information you have?"

"My main concern is to make sure we can cope with the situation we have been saddled with. At present we are looking at what we have and what we can do with it. How the Heathrow incident happened will have to be dealt with later. It is embedded and cannot be changed; the future is our prime concern. I can say that Heathrow cannot be cleaned up and back in operation in a few days. It may take a few years. It will take something like a year just to clear the site, and it will take years to locate, identify and tag all the dead bodies. The first estimate of the number of dead is between 25,000 and 35,000. That may prove to be a very conservative estimate. We have not yet started to evacuate the tunnels or the Underground network. We have at least 10,000 casualties in hospitals, including temporary hospitals, and we have another 5,000 being treated at their homes because we don't have enough hospital beds. At least another 10,000 to 20,000 are unaccounted for, so we could be looking at a total of some 50,000-plus dead. We have drafted in the army to secure the area, and the army, air force and navy are using their expertise in crash-site management. We will have to liaise with private construction companies as well as the original builders and architects, but our main priority is to clear the site. We will also be liaising with the Americans regarding the experience they gained through the Twin Towers disaster in New York. Yet another cause for concern is that we are not yet fully aware of how many foreign nationals were at Heathrow at the time – not just passengers, but airline and airport staff. Persons from all over the UK were probably there for catching flights or meeting friends and family. It will probably take many years to obtain and catalogue all the data of just the persons who are already deceased; we will probably have more fatalities among those in hospitals at present. Other persons may live for some time, but then die from their injuries; so the final death toll may not be available for decades."

"Building Minister, your input please?"

"Like the rest of you, I was deeply affected by the sight of the disaster at Heathrow. It is not possible to imagine the horror. Before I walked on to the site, I could not comprehend what had happened. It wasn't like visiting a building site. Terminal 5 just a short time ago was open and was celebrated as an amazing space-age structure – a building that struck people with total amazement and awe – but there I was, looking at a smouldering, smoking major disaster. There was a sickening stench – a stench I had never ever come across before in my life. I was stumbling over burnt-out bodies, some in piles that had become fused together in the heat. I could hardly identify what I saw as people. Terminals 1, 2 and 3 are in a similar condition, above and below ground. The basement and tunnel areas are a black hole of gloom. It is a disaster of unimaginable magnitude. How do you clear a site of 50,000 bodies, numerous burnt-out buildings and so much destroyed infrastructure? Imagine how long it will take and how many people will be required. It isn't just a case of picking up bodies one by one. How do you cope with several bodies welded together? How do you identify them? Think how bad it seemed when fifty persons were killed by bombs in London, and think of the effect it had on the Americans when 3,000 lives were lost during 9/11. How will the country react when they hear that 50,000 have died? Hundreds turn out when bodies of soldiers are returned from overseas. Just how long would you have to stand in the rain as 50,000 coffins go by? How long would it take to identify, cremate or bury 50,000 bodies? Just how many years would that take? Some 10,000 attend the Remembrance Day parade in London for the Great War of seventy years past. Will we now have another Remembrance Day with probably half a million or more attending? We don't have a church or cathedral big enough in the UK.

"Acting Foreign Secretary, can we have your input, please?"

"We have been working with the CIA, but they are more concerned about protecting the USA. They are trawling desperately to find out the whys and hows, especially as they actually considered a terrorist attack at Heathrow but did not realise just how easily it could happen, or how major it would be. Security was in place to spot would-be hijackers, but there was no security in place at Heathrow that could have prevented what happened. The security system was in place to apprehend any persons attempting to use rockets to bring down planes on the flight path approaching Heathrow, but in this case the cause was inside the perimeter of the airport. Why the perpetrators were not apprehended is something we need to look into. At present we have no evidence that terrorists on the ground were responsible for the disaster, or that terrorists were on board either of the two planes which crashed. The SAS found and killed four terrorists in the maintenance terminal building, but there is no firm evidence that they caused the carnage of Heathrow, or even that they were related to the group at Buckingham Palace. However, we have been able to establish that the ambulance and the UPS van found at Buckingham Palace had come from Heathrow, but how and why have not been established yet. I am ashamed to say that we still do not have a plausible answer. All we can do is continue to investigate. Maybe some organisation will claim responsibility. I can say there is a worldwide search under way for the terrorists, but it is like looking for a needle in a haystack. The chance of finding the needle would be better probably. Not only that, but if we find those responsible, what will we do – hang them? What good will that be? We need to shut the gate before the horse can bolt. It's simple common sense. It is not common sense to send your army to a foreign country to kill farmers and warlords when the people who can hurt you most are in your backyard. Surely the amount of money and effort it takes to attack the people in Afghanistan should be spent in protecting our own borders. The persons who have been killed in Afghanistan had not left their country to attack us; they convinced others to do that for them. In Iraq Saddam was removed, but now the country is in a worse state. There have been more Iraqis killed since he was removed than when he was in charge. When we all leave Afghanistan the same will probably happen."

"General, can we have your information please?"

"The army and other forces' top brass are very worried about damage to the morale of soldiers serving overseas when they see TV pictures of parts of the UK, their homeland, being attacked and destroyed. They are putting forward a case for the immediate strategic withdrawal of the army based in Afghanistan, as they believe they could be better employed rebuilding and protecting their homeland. The enlisted men are very worried not just about the damaged to the UK, but also about the safety of their loved ones. Some of the men are anxiously awaiting news of family and friends who live or work in the London area. They are demanding to return home to fight the terrorists on our own soil. The top brass are finding it very difficult to justify why they are over there when the immediate danger is back at home. The situation is getting extremely difficult. We are asking men to go out in the wilderness and look for bombs hidden in roadside ditches, knowing they have been put there to kill them. They know full well that if they were not in the country the problem wouldn't be there. As one captain said, we are needed at home, not here. Enough is enough. We can defend our country; the politicians can't even defend themselves, let alone watch our backs and keep our home base secure and our families safe."

"Education Secretary, can you add your thoughts?"

"We are working with the schools, and we have drafted in extra manpower to help us cope with the problems we are experiencing, which are well beyond our normal capabilities. We have been swamped by the sheer number of health and mental problems experienced by primary and secondary teachers and pupils. Many children have lost friends and family members. Some have become orphans. We ourselves are finding it very difficult, even impossible, to cope with the situation, let alone come to terms with what has happened. We don't have enough resources, and we are not knowledgeable enough to handle this problem. Secondary schools have the same problems. Just because the children are older doesn't mean they can cope any more easily. This is all about human beings. Age is immaterial. We suddenly have the very world we live in just smashed to pieces, and friends, families, generations wiped out by some madmen motivated by their ideology of world rule. At this moment my anger is directed at the Americans and all those who support them. How dare they? How dare they cause this trauma and destroy the lives of thousands of our innocent children? Let me go on: we now have thousands of children so traumatised that they are likely to grow up into persons who hate the world and become avengers themselves. I will not apologise for my outburst – not to any man present at this meeting, Thank you all for listening."

"Education Secretary, thank you. Thank you for having the courage to tell us your personal feelings. I think I can say, for every person here, that your spoken feelings are the feelings of us all, but we didn't have the same courage to speak out. Any apologies should come from us and not you."

"Health Secretary, I expect you have a vast number of comments?"

"My answer to what has happened in the last days is simple. I put my arms up and scream. I scream for help because, my God, we need a hell of a lot of help. Every hospital in the country is on high alert – not just because of Heathrow, but also because prior to Heathrow we were overloaded with the norovirus epidemic. They have had to abandon their previous way of operating, and they all have been totally traumatised by the huge numbers of casualties. They are now overflowing. Many of the hospitals have had to reopen previously closed wards, and cancel planned operations and clinics. The hospitals' managements are asking about the extra costing and if government performance targets have been shelved for the time being. They say they cannot possibly meet the existing targets. Their scheduled patients will have to wait longer for their appointments and operations. Their complete system has been hijacked by this event, and it will take many months, years, to clear the resulting backlog of patients. We also have to consider the thousands of persons who will need aftercare and attention, artificial limbs, plastic surgery, mobility aids and special housing. A vast number of persons have damaged eyesight and other defects requiring treatment and convalescent homes. Almost every county in the country will have to provide these extra services just at a time when they have been forced to make so many reductions to their budgets. We, the government, need to look again at the country in a totally different light. We need to see if the extra funding can be provided by Brussels. Do they have a contingency plan and is aid available for this sort of disaster? They may decide that we should get no support, but that any country in similar need in the future will be protected."

"Special forces, your report please."

"At airports the scanning machines are there to detect the mini terrorist – the odd person who wants to cause a stir, maybe create some damage or bring down a plane to prove a point. Typically he is a person who has a bad life and is jealous of others. He has no job, no big house, no big car. He doesn't see the point of the next forty years. He wants to end his life, but he decides to do so in a way that means he will be remembered. The media have set him the agenda by their methods of reporting. One day they will realise that if the media didn't exist, then not so many persons would carry out atrocities. There would be no reason, as no one would know. You could say that the best weapon a terrorist has is the media, and not his gun or his bomb. If they knew their last video of martyrdom would be burnt and never looked at, there would be no point in their carrying out their bombing. We should take into account that the security system at Heathrow was designed to prevent terrorists from boarding planes and taking off. If this incident was caused by planes landing at Heathrow, then our security was useless and our losses could be a result of another country's security failure. Our security may be good enough to protect other countries – good for them – but what about us? Yes, for God's sake, what about us? We need a total overhaul of all our operational procedures and all our security systems need to be run correctly and safely, not controlled by ineffective private companies where profit is of a higher priority than public and country safety. We should bloody well remember the Olympics security saga and learn from it – and learn damn quick. The Olympics were a success because we did not have a terrorist visit, and not because our security was so good and effective. The rapid-response team based adjacent to the palace was ineffective, and any experience and first-hand knowledge of their encounter with the terrorists has gone with them to their graves so cannot be passed on to others. We need to have the unit within the palace perimeter and not outside to ensure we can respond before and not after the event."

"Ministers, from my observations of the reports from all your departments, it would seem that the rebuilding of Heathrow is not as important as the rebuilding of the persons of our nation. Our number-one priority should be to use all our available resources and knowledge to rebuild the people's lives and their confidence, rather than Heathrow. It will take all our available resources. We have to treat every single body with dignity, and we must give adequate support to the probable 250,000 grieving relatives. We will have to establish a dialogue with the Americans to benefit from the experience and knowledge they gained from 9/11 and the way they rebuilt the area around the Twin Towers. It might mean that Heathrow will have to be rebuilt in a totally different way – more of a memorial site than an airport. We may have to accept exactly what the persons of this country vote on, and not what is better for the private sector and their money-making ideas.

An important lesson for us is that close to a major city is not the safest location for an airport unless you can guarantee security at all times. Because of the proximity of Heathrow to the city of London we could have ended up with both the airport and the city wiped out, and we might have had to hold this meeting in a cowshed upcountry. We have to consider the consequences of having the country's main control centre in London. Have we placed all our eggs in one basket? Could we survive if we lost London instead of Heathrow? Could that plane have crashed into this building? If it had, what would be the outcome? We need to set up a very good think tank which is able to come up with solutions to cover all eventualities. If we can't find solutions, we might not have a future."

CHAPTER EIGHT

Heathrow, the Aftermath

How did it happen? How could it happen?

A cargo plane was transporting live animals from Berlin Zoo to London Zoo. Two qualified veterinary surgeons from the Berlin Zoo were travelling with the cargo, and they had instructions to tranquillise the animals if they became a danger to the safety of the plane.

On approaching Heathrow and joining the spiral landing stack, the pilot made emergency contact with air traffic control and stated that the co-pilot was having a heart attack. So air traffic control arranged for the plane to bypass the stack and spiral and enter Heathrow's landing corridor. The control tower at Heathrow arranged for an ambulance and paramedics to be at the cargo terminal to meet the plane.

The plane landed and taxied to the cargo terminal, and the paramedics rushed on to the plane to stabilise the co-pilot. The pilot and navigator left the plane as normal, but the two veterinary surgeons stayed with the plane, and they 'dealt with' the two paramedics. The crates carrying the animals were unloaded by the normal ground personnel and put inside a warehouse to await the arrival of the people from London Zoo. Because the plane had arrived early, they were not yet at the terminal. When they did arrive, they too were 'dealt with', and their bodies were concealed in the empty animal crates. The two Berlin Zoo veterinary surgeons were bogus. They left the plane dressed as paramedics, carrying the stretchered co-pilot and loaded him on board the parked ambulance. Then they drove to the terminal warehouse and entered. They opened the unloaded crates to let out the terrorists concealed inside with their weapons of mass disruption and destruction. All other persons in the terminal buildings were disabled silently by the use of the tranquilliser guns the sham veterinary surgeons were carrying. The tranquilliser drug was powerful enough to knock out an elephant and could be used to kill a human being quickly and silently.

The terrorists then dispersed wearing normal UK police uniforms, and four of them went to the refuelling unit and disposed of the personnel there. No alarm was raised because nothing appeared to be wrong. There were no loud bangs or screams.

Two oil tankers left the unit. One went to the end of the runway, just inside the perimeter fence, and parked there. Still nothing appeared wrong. Nothing had been discovered at the cargo warehouse or refuelling unit, and no notice had been taken of the two oil tankers making their way around the airport.

At that moment a Boeing 747 jumbo jet was approaching the runway. The pilot, because of limited ground vision, owing to his position in the cabin, didn't notice the tanker. The plane was travelling at almost 200 mph with landing gear and wing flaps down. On the far side of the tanker the terrorists were now standing on the airport side of the truck, concealed from any prying eyes on the perimeter roadway. The terrorists had a rocket launcher resting on the top of the truck.

The plane was just passing over the perimeter fence when the rocket was fired, accurately. The terrorists had had months of training and preparing. The rocket travelled at a trajectory of less than thirty degrees, so it was not noticeable as a rocket fired vertically would be, and it entered the air intake of the port engine. It was an easy target, as the engine sucked the rocket in. The explosion wrecked the port wing and the outer port engine and ripped apart the inner port engine. The sudden dramatic loss of balance and lack of wing support and power caused the two starboard engines to pull their wing upward in a cartwheel motion, and the plane veered to port. The pilot lost all control of the plane, and within a split second it had hurtled across the sky and crashed into Terminal 5 and its satellite buildings at 200 mph.

Some of the aeroplanes parked at the terminals were full of passengers and had full fuel tanks. If you consider the damage that just two planes with fuel caused to the Twin Towers in the 9/11 disaster, then just think of the devastation when eight aeroplanes full of fuel exploded beside the terminal buildings.

The terrorists who had brought down that plane now drove their tankers to another part of the airport and used their hand-held RPG to destroy the two control towers. Because now the focus of the airport personnel was towards the Terminal 5 area, nobody took any notice of the two tankers and two security cars. The two tankers seemed to be moving towards the storage tanks to refuel – just a normal procedure.

All the airport emergency services stood still in total shock for a few minutes. This was not on their list of possibilities. They had expected at the very most a plane belly-flopping on the runway, or a plane landing on the runway with an engine on fire, so where did this nightmare come from? Which training manual covered an event like this? Or were they just watching a film?

After the fact that they had a major incident had sunk in, the emergency vehicles began to respond. They raced towards the blazing Terminal 5 complex. They were now approaching a virtual wall of fire, and they were about to be trapped by another wall of fire when the second plane crashed to the ground behind them. Rapidly forming lagoons of fuel from ruptured petrol tanks ignited and formed flames of death. Within just a few minutes the emergency personnel and their vehicles were engulfed and destroyed. Almost all the airport's emergency services were eliminated and removed from the equation. The flames and smoke from the burning runway, terminal buildings and planes were being fanned by aeroplanes which were flying in and aborting their landings, and the inferno roared towards the other terminals. Planes taxiing out for take-off, loaded with high-octane fuel, were unable to escape. One of them had just left the ground when it was engulfed by flames and converted into a flying bomb, totally out of control, with immense destructive power.

When air traffic control lost contact with the Heathrow control tower, they assumed a computer glitch was to blame and expected them to be back on line shortly. In the meantime other passenger planes were making their approach to land at approximately two-minute interval. The pilots of the second plane noticed the fire as they approached the runway and tried to contact the control tower, but there was no reply. The pilot contacted air traffic control, who knew of no reason why he should abort. They asked the pilot if he could see if the runway was clear, and when he replied that it was they told him to go ahead. The fire looked serious, but it didn't seem necessary to abort the landing.

The pilot was close to the ground when he noticed the high-octane kerosene on the Tarmac in front of him. For his aeroplane and the totally entrapped passengers it was too late.

The two fuel tankers driven by the terrorists had moved to the side of the runway and had opened fully their fuel valves so that the high-octane kerosene was like a gushing river flowing across the runway. When the aeroplane's tyres reached the oily fuel they lost grip and the plane veered out of control. At the same time the terrorists ignited the fuel, and a fireball engulfed the plane. Because the plane's engines were still rotating, the burning fuel was sucked in and flames were blown out from the rear of the engine like the flames from a rocket engine. The fuselage was scorched and melted on both sides, and the plane flopped on to the ground and skidded along, engulfed by burning fuel. It was as though a toy plane had been thrown into a crematorium oven. In a matter of five minutes two catastrophic incidents had occurred at Heathrow and no one knew the terrorists were even there. Everyone put it down as a tragic accident.

The emergency services at the airport were going through their normal procedure from their training books but as they raced towards the fire they were gobsmacked by the scale of the disaster. They wondered how they would be able to tackle a blaze of such catastrophic proportions.

The normal emergency chain of command was broken in places by communication failure and lack of knowledge and experience. They were initially drawn to Terminal 5, but behind their backs another major incident occurred at that moment. Their well-rehearsed emergency procedure was totally shattered.

Still no one had taken any notice of the terrorists who were loose within the airport. They attracted no attention. They were not running around, screaming and firing guns. They were not dressed like the kind of terrorist shown on TV or in films. How would you ever notice anything different was taking place among the 70,000 or 80,000 persons who work at Heathrow. The terrorists would seem to be just normal persons going about their daily routine, and they would be able to create any mayhem they wanted to. If any genuine airport employee bumped into someone in police uniform, it wouldn't occur to the employee that the 'policeman' was anything other than his uniform proclaimed him to be. Nobody was likely to challenge him.

When the crash happened there were no air-raid sirens, no klaxons. Heathrow at that moment was a place you didn't want to be. Shouts and screams split the air waves as exploding fireballs leapt skywards and the aluminium bodies of planes tore and exploded. Searing, searching fingers of burning kerosene raced across the ground like channels of lava, devouring angrily everything in their path. The rivers and walls of flame were everywhere. The terrorists, after opening the valves on the fuel tankers, had also opened all the valves on the main fuel storage tanks, so Heathrow was becoming awash with millions of gallons of high-octane highly volatile aeroplane fuel, kerosene. The terrorists were in control at Heathrow. There was nobody opposing their carnage. We did not have a Rambo. They could have just packed up and left Heathrow, and nobody would have been the wiser for days or months. Heathrow wasn't just an Underground station, a small pocket of people being bombed by a small explosive (even that small incident caused the London emergency services and A & E departments a major problem). Heathrow was like a working city with 80,000 workers and 1,500 passengers each day. Two hundred aeroplanes were on the ground and 100 were in the air in the spiral stack. The nightmare was caused by just a few persons in a crowd of thousands.

The line of aeroplanes from the terminals were taxiing out to the runway for take-off, and the pilots were busy checking their instruments. They saw no reason to abort and took no notice of the two fuel tankers driving along the side of the runway. The terrorists had deliberately placed themselves on the port side of the aeroplanes as this was the side the doors were usually on. They then opened the tankers' fuel valves and drove along with the planes so that the fuel ran across the runway. They then ignited the fuel. The first the pilots of the first aeroplane in the queue noticed was when his tyres exploded and the aeroplane dropped forward as though it was in a drunken stupor. When the aeroplane came to a halt, the pilot was still unaware of what had happened. He shut down the engines and tried to alert the control tower, but both the control towers had been destroyed, so no alert was passed on. The emergency communication system had already been destroyed. The slowly revolving engines sucked in the flames and sprayed the flames and fuel like a blowlamp from the engine's rear. Only then did the pilot look out at the wing and notice the flames. Even so, he assumed it was a system failure and started to go thought the normal procedure for an engine fire. The co-pilot alerted the cabin staff to arrange the evacuation procedure, not realising that a fire was burning directly underneath the main fuselage – an area that cannot be seen from within the aircraft.

The pilot of the next aeroplane in the queue could see the difficulties of the aeroplane in front, but he did not think he was in any danger. He just stopped and tried to contact the control tower, but had no response. While he waited for instructions his aircraft started to burn, and it wasn't long before four aeroplanes were suffering the same difficulties. The last two aeroplanes in the queue turned off the runway and ran on to the grass to avoid the river of fire heading towards them. The first four planes had tried to evacuate, but when the door opened and the emergency chutes dropped down to the ground they caught fire and the fire raced up towards the open doors. The quick-thinking crews tried to close the doors (not an easy task with the chute in the way), and some were badly burnt in the operation. The planes quickly filled with acrid smoke while the crew rushed round helping passengers with the oxygen masks, and the pilots frantically tried to come up with a solution. They were in an unprecedented situation, so no operational procedure existed. They hoped that the emergency services would be there quickly and foam would be used to extinguish the fire, so they sat tight and waited. The cabin crew tried to reassure the passengers as they also believed help was coming quickly.

The two planes which had left the runway were following normal evacuate procedure, but when they opened their doors the acrid smoke was sucked into the plane fuselage by the pressure difference and the air-conditioning system. Nevertheless the evacuation chutes were deployed and they carried out passenger evacuation. Soon there were about 400 or 500 persons at ground level, startled, frightened, stressed and panicking, frantically looking round them. All they could see was fires burning and constant fireballs as explosions happened all around. It was a truly frightening environment compared with the cabin they had just left, and there seemed no safe haven to make their way to. The cabin crew, again believing that the emergency services would be there quickly, asked the passengers to sit on the ground to avoid the acrid smoke. They were unaware that fires were also burning beneath them, underground, and at any moment they could be blown sky-high by gas and fuel explosions. Everybody was frantically using mobile phones to call friends and family, which spread even more panic outside the airport and caused more persons to jump in their cars and head for Heathrow. There was a mass migration of persons heading into the disaster zone, to compound the already escalating crisis caused by too many bodies on the ground.

At no point, from the start to the finish of these few minutes, had anybody realised that the cause was terrorist activity. There had been no warning of the approaching danger. The normal person, the security services and the armed police had been going about their daily work as normal, and because of the physical size of Heathrow a few extra normal-looking persons on the ground did not attract any adverse attention.

Had a person appeared who looked like the typical terrorist, as featured on the TV or in films, he would have been noticed and dealt with, but when the airport was suddenly turned into a catastrophic crash scene no thought was given to the possibility that terrorists were involved. Everybody's attention was focused on survival. In just a short few minutes, Heathrow, the nation's heartbeat, had stopped. It had been changed into the nation's crematorium. The situation was far worse than anything in the archives of world wars. In the future the world will see archive photos of scenes far worse than those in the Nazi concentration camps of Poland, and it will be described how, in just a few minutes, England became another Ground Zero. Another emergency operation of amazing magnitude began, and it would make the Blitz in any city during the Second World War shrink and fade in comparison. Heathrow would be catapulted to the top of the world rankings of the worst world disasters of all time.

When the third plane approached the runway just two minutes after the second, the pilot could see the runway was on fire but could not see that the plane in front had crash-landed. He took evasive action, aborted landing and notified air traffic control. Air traffic control now had the problem of working out a revised programme. They had a plane which they had assumed was landing, but it would now need instructions to return to the stack. From what the pilot had told them, they still did not know if the next plane could land. They had no contact with Heathrow, so they asked the pilot of the next approaching plane to abort landing unless he could see clear space. The pilot aborted his landing and gave his reasons to air traffic control, so they told the pilots of all the other planes in the landing corridor to abort. The aborting planes flew over Heathrow, and so the draughts and turbulence from the engines as they increased power caused a high-pressure wind that fanned the fires on the ground to a much higher temperature.

Now air traffic control had the problem of a spiral stack of aeroplanes with nowhere to land. Every two minutes another plane was arriving from another distant location and entering the top of the stack, expecting to spiral down to the landing corridor. This was not a TV programme – it was real. There were no adverts – real live people were being cremated by the thousand, by the tens of thousands. Now the aeroplanes at the bottom of the stack, who should have been leaving the stack and entering the landing corridor, had to be directed to head back to the top of the stack again. More aeroplanes were entering at the top than were leaving at the bottom. There were four stacks, and they were quickly becoming taller. Other stacks were formed. The situation was like a water tap filling a sink. The water should drain down the plughole; but if you put the plug in, the water fills the sink and overflows. If you have four taps with only one drain, the problem is worse. Air traffic control had to work back from Heathrow to prevent planes taking off bound for Heathrow. The planes already in the air had to be diverted, taking into account the fuel levels, size and weight of the aircraft as not all other airports can safely accept the larger planes. It was far more important to consider the aeroplanes' landing capabilities than how many passengers the airport could cope with or even if the plane could take off again. At that moment every available runway was needed, and that might mean motorways had to be closed off and used. Planes with enough fuel were diverted to land somewhere in Europe.

The black toxic clouds were engulfing the other terminals and the crisis was exacerbated when lights began going out everywhere. Heathrow had become a black, toxic, fireball meltdown of biblical proportions. It seemed to have risen from the deep, dark caverns of hell, and yet the world outside Heathrow was unaware of how bad the situation was. Persons were still making their way to view the spectacle as it unfolded. They did not imagine how vast the area was or what an enormous number of people were involved. No one could think that a few people could cause so much damage and loss of life to 100,000 people in just a few minutes. At first there was no reason to believe it was any more serious than other accidents that they had seen reported on TV. The media helicopter had been shot down by the terrorists using their RPG, but that was not known. The general view was that there had been some sort of engine or rotor failure. No one had imagined that what had happened at Heathrow was like a scene from the film *Blackhawk Down*, but without prewarning. That was just a film, and not reality, but had the terrorists watched that film and used it as a training manual? The first TV pictures did not give a full picture of the devastation that had happened in a few short minutes or give any clue about the cause. It wouldn't be long before TV crews would be setting up at vantage points beside the perimeter fences, and spectators would be opening their cans and eating their sweets as they stood and watched. Yet they would have run screaming, trampling each other, if the terrorists had suddenly appeared and turned their weapons on the thrill-seekers.

Below ground level was another scene of carnage, which the persons at ground level were totally unaware of. The rivulets of fuel that had hungrily gobbled their way across the virgin ground drained through ventilation shafts into the tunnels which ran between the terminals, as well into as the tunnel of the Underground train system. In the train tunnel electric sparks ignited the leaking fuel, and the draught from the trains and the ventilation system caused a fireball to sweep down the tunnel, engulfing an approaching train. The train ground to a halt and the passengers, with nowhere to go, were burnt and gassed alive trapped in their crushed metal can.

In the road tunnel vehicles suddenly drove into a wall of fire and intense heat. They crashed into one another and the flames and fumes were assisted by fuel from split vehicle tanks. The pressure and temperature build-up in the tunnels was enormous.

Flames and smoke were forced to escape upwards from the Underground system by way of lift shafts, escalators and ventilation ducts, spreading into other terminals and the bus station. People were thrown aside and trampled on as they frantically tried to escape, but there was no escape. Everywhere there was screaming, burning persons. Soon the casualties outnumbered the uninjured by 1,000 to one. The very air they needed to breathe was sucked out of their lungs and vaporised by the intensity of the raging fireballs. Before long the area was littered with piles of burnt flesh and bones, fused together by the heat. Persons had the skin blasted from their bones by jets of red-hot steam and red-hot liquid metal as water pipes melted in the intense heat.

Outside the buildings, vehicles trying to escape from the airport had crashed in the main exit tunnel and caused a blockage, so other vehicles had tried to escape via the adjacent entry tunnel. This had caused more crashes, so both sides of the main tunnel into and out of the airport were blocked with burning vehicles. In the service and maintenance tunnels wiring and piping had burnt and melted. The fractured gas supply pipes were turned into lances and cut through the lines of communication and electricity. The infrastructure of Heathrow Airport was being destroyed piece by piece, block by block, inch by inch.

In the Underground, the hellfire caverns would burn for weeks, repeatedly petering out and restarting with even more vigour. Flames raged angrily through the air, whipping with violence and fury as if in defiance of mankind and as if with the specific intent of causing never-ending carnage.

Having caused the carnage and devastation, the terrorists were now heading for their second objective. They regrouped at the maintenance terminal, quickly entered and took over the main building, which was almost empty of personnel because they had been drawn towards the carnage taking place in other parts of the airport. The terrorists set up two-man HMG and RPG units in the second-floor rooms at each end of the building. Then three of them lifted a device from their vehicle and, using the office-block lift, made their way up to the top floor using the fire-escape stairs and on to the roof.

The terrorists noticed a group of four men in the area between their building and the building opposite and realised they were armed men and a possible threat, so both terrorist units opened fire with their RPG, which hit the Tarmac close to the four men. They immediately dispersed behind the parked vehicles between them and the terrorists, who then fired using their HMG. The four men were pinned down and unable to move from their location, whereas the terrorists had a brilliant high vantage point. They were in total control. One of the armed men had both his legs severely damaged by concrete fragments sent up by the explosion as the RPG exploded on the Tarmac. He was receiving first aid from the leader, Troll, while the other two covered them and returned fire at the terrorists. Troll, realising the gravity of their situation, made contact with

Sheppard, the SAS operations officer at their base at RAF Northolt. He disclosed their compromised position and requested urgent assistance.

Some time later the crates containing the live animals which had been earmarked for delivery to Heathrow were found still at the cargo warehouse in the airport at Berlin. This discovery was not instantly related to the happening at Heathrow. It would take months before the details were put together. Somehow the terrorists had overcome the real veterinary surgeons, who were found dead and hidden away near where the animals were found. The animals were only noticed when the warehouse staff were disturbed by the noise as the animals became hungry and wanted feeding. It was then realised that the crates loaded on to the aeroplane must have been the wrong ones. Even then it was assumed that it had been a simple mistake. The two real veterinary surgeons found dead were not immediately identified as murder victims as they had no visible injuries. They had to be autopsied before the causes of death were established. It wasn't until some time later, when the missing empty crates were found at Heathrow, that the idea was put forward that the original animal crates had been deliberately swapped for ones containing terrorists, but there would never be any actual evidence to prove that was what happened on that day. The two bogus veterinary surgeons had been accepted as genuine by the flight crew because of the animals. They were not known personally to the flight crew, and no one suspected a thing. They had become friendly with the crew during the flight and had put a drug in the co-pilot's drink, which caused symptoms similar to a heart attack, but that too would never be proved as the co-pilot's body was never found. The pilot and flight engineer, who had left Heathrow just before the start of the carnage, were both interviewed and interrogated by police from all the countries involved, but nothing out of the ordinary was found; and despite their viewing thousands of photos, they were not able to identify the terrorists. Air traffic control had not suspected that the plane had been hijacked, because it had not. It appeared to be just a normal cargo flight carrying live animals for London Zoo. When they arrived at Heathrow, the animals should have been put into quarantine, so the aeroplane was met by animal welfare officers rather than armed security.

No one at the cargo terminal was expecting a heavily armed human cargo, so the terrorists were able to overcome the terminal personnel without detection, to load their commandeered vehicles with their weapons, and to make their way across the airport without being challenged. Their presence, at this stage, gave no cause for concern.

Another section of the terrorist group took over the ambulance provided for the co-pilot. Two of the terrorists were dressed as ambulance men and one terrorist lay on the stretcher dressed in the co-pilot's uniform. Also a UPS van that had been waiting for a delivery was loaded with weapons and other items. The ambulance then moved away with its blue lights on. So as not to attract suspicion, the driver used the siren only when necessary to persuade drivers of other vehicles to move over, and he was able to make an uninterrupted fifteen-mile journey along the A4 motorway and the West Way into London, followed closely by the brown UPS delivery van. This 'convoy' did not attract suspicion and the ambulance siren helped to clear a way through the traffic.

The officers at the gates of Buckingham Palace were surprised by the arrival of the ambulance, but they assumed that someone in the palace had phoned for it. Their only concern was that they didn't cause a delay. The two ambulance men easily distracted the officers, who were then overpowered by terrorists from the UPS van, which had stopped behind the ambulance. The brown UPS van seemed to be a normal palace delivery van and did not attract any suspicion, and the ambulance and van blocked the view from the palace as the officers were overpowered. The ambulance then moved forward, as did the brown UPS van, to the entrance to the main building, where it was out of view from the road and gateway. The two ambulance men then entered the main building carrying their medical bag.

The first impression of the two armed officers of the royal

protection unit was that two normal ambulance men were approaching. Having heard the siren, they assumed that somebody in the building had phoned for an ambulance and the two ambulance men had entered through the main front door because they did not know where in the building their service was required. The officers were easily disarmed and 'dealt with'.

The other terrorists then entered the building and carried out a 'search and seek' operation. From outside the palace, everything seemed quite normal. The parked ambulance did not cause much concern. If a passing reporter had stopped to ask whom the ambulance was for, he or she would have been fobbed off by the terrorists at the gate now masquerading as police officers (the bodies of the real officers were now concealed in the brown UPS van). At that moment the focus of the media was being drawn by the aeroplane crash at Heathrow, so the happenings at the palace did not attract any media attention.

CHAPTER NINE

"Secretary, I believe you have some information to disclose?"

"Yes. Because of the crisis the Heathrow disaster has caused, we in the civil service have formed a completely new department made up of several crucial sections. Each section has a head and these heads will liaise together as a committee in order to evaluate and distribute information to the appropriate departments and ministers. Two persons head the department, and they have direct access to me, and to you as, the Acting Prime Minister. I suggest they attend Cabinet meetings and be responsible for updating Parliament. This new department has been created because of the complex nature of the data arising from the disaster, which covers a vast area. Thus we need persons who are knowledgeable and experienced civil servants, preferably with a legal background. One section is responsible for collecting details of all the persons who were killed. That in itself will be an enormous task. We will have to record race, religion and nationality. This will take considerable time and resources. Another section is dealing with the support required by relations of the deceased. I am sure you all can imagine the complex nature of this section. Some victims may have just a single relation; others may have an enormous number of young children and other dependants. We already know that many children have become orphans. Yet another section is dealing with insurance and compensation. This section is divided into two, one covering the UK and the other covering foreign countries. Another section, also divided into two, is dealing with the clearing of the Heathrow site and the rebuilding of Heathrow and its infrastructure.

"We have designated Gatwick as the replacement for Heathrow, and we are restructuring its management and employing extra personnel. Road and rail links into London are being improved. We have had meetings with the councils in the Gatwick area, they assure us that they can cope with the extra burden on their infrastructure and resources.

"Regarding worldwide air travel, Britain's capacity has been reduced by some fifty per cent, and we are looking for ways of increasing that by upgrading some of our smaller airports and reopening closed ones.

"We are fortunate that the main road-transport network has not been damaged. All the roads to Heathrow are now open. Also we are working to clear a runway so we can safely remove any serviceable aircraft. The owners can arrange for them to be used at other airports. When they are all removed, we can use the runway to airlift items in and out as required."

CHAPTER TEN

A special meeting authorised by the heads of MI5 and MI6 was attended by their section leaders and Colonel Sheppard and Major Viper of the SAS regiment – two persons involved with the Heathrow crisis.

"Gentlemen, we have called this meeting for two reasons: so that we may hear the first report of the Heathrow disaster and to look at the detailed information collated by Major Viper regarding the terrorists' methods. The destruction of Heathrow has shown us that we need better intelligence-gathering. The terrorists might have added 6 million more deaths to the thousands lost at Heathrow and we ourselves might have been added to the list, and the world might have been looking at a country which had become a burnt-out wasteland. The CIA admit that the Twin Towers disaster was a drop in the ocean compared with what might happen if the terrorists attack New York in the same way as they did Heathrow. If they deploy chemical weapons, then the lights will go out very quickly. It is our job to prevent that happening. Colonel, Major, in line with out normal protocol, no minutes or recordings will be made of this meeting. Colonel Sheppard, can you give us any ideas you may have about just how the incident at Heathrow came about?"

"Sirs, no organisation has yet claimed responsibility. We believe that is because the persons responsible have not yet returned to their base."

"Colonel, don't you feel they would have admitted responsibility straight away if they were going to?"

"No, sir. It's likely that the ringleader actually took part in the operation and would like to be the one who is acclaimed. When he gets back to his base he will receive a hero's welcome, and he will want to broadcast an announcement to the world."

"I see, Colonel. Please carry on."

"As has been said, we are slowly putting together information. The evidence we have leads us to believe that an inbound Boeing 747 jumbo caused the destruction of the new Terminal 5 satellite complex. This was compounded by the destruction of the Underground network, that being caused by thousands of gallons of leaking fuel, which also caused an inferno to spread through the other airport terminals. The reason the Boeing 747 veered off course seems to be an explosion on the port wing engine. This has been confirmed by several witnesses. Why the explosion? We can only make guesses. One possibility is that a bomb was placed on the plane. How or by whom, we don't yet know."

"Colonel, how do you think it was detonated. From someone on board – a sort of suicide bomber?"

"Sir, that is a possibility; but if so, it was more by luck than judgement that it hit the terminal. Another possibility is based on the recent discovery of a body on the ground. Because of its location and its frozen state, the dead man was thought to have been a stowaway in the landing wheel space of a plane. The body had frozen during the trip and, on approach to landing, when the wheels were lowered, the body fell out. Now, straight after that body was discovered visual inspection of planes' wheel areas became routine. I don't know if any of you have ever seen the retracted wheel area of a typical Boeing 747. It is a vast cavity, and a stowaway could be missed. The area ought to be scanned with X-ray equipment, but that would be time-consuming and expensive. The wheel cavities are only sealed off after take-off, and it is virtually impossible to keep them under surveillance until then. Nevertheless, it would be easier to detect a person concealed in that area than to detect a package designed to look like a piece of normal apparatus. Pressure-operated devices are ideal terrorist weapons. No terrorist would need to be on the plane."

"Colonel, can you elaborate on the pressure device, please?"

"Well, a small cylindrical device made to look like a hydraulic unit could be concealed in the nose wheel cavity of any plane. It could be detonated by a simple pressure-operated switch. This could be activated when the plane reaches its normal cruising height of, say, 30,000 feet; then when the plane comes down to land the device will detonate when the plane descends to, say, 100 feet, or even ground level. The nose wheel area is directly below the cockpit, so the hydraulics and electrical systems would be damaged and the pilots would lose control of the plane."

"Colonel, I follow your explanation, but the end result would be unpredictable, don't you think?"

"That's right. I believe that when all is revealed the disaster at Heathrow will be found to contain a high degree of luck, rather than amazing strategic planning. At the same time, the world's terrorists have access to a vast amount of information that we in the West publicise, and I feel they will become more scientific in their approach. Every time we read about a new scientific development we ask ourselves how we can use it for our own ends; so do they. The Germans were the first to use aeroplanes to bomb cities; then came the pilotless flying bomb. Now the technology is freely available, so could the terrorist design a plane in which, like the flying bomb, the fuel would cut off after the plane has covered a certain distance, so the plane will just fall out of the sky. It could be raining planes on the cities of the world. A major obstacle to our obtaining accurate details of the incident at Heathrow is the physical damage to the equipment and buildings and the planes themselves. We do know there were terrorists on the ground, but were they there before or after the first plane crashed? Did they cause that themselves, or was their visit unrelated? We do know that they had and were capable of using RPG rockets, but we don't know how many times they used their rockets, if at all. We do know from witness accounts that the two control towers were destroyed by explosions. Was it a suicide bomber inside the building or an external rocket attack? It will take considerable forensics examination before we have the answer to that question. It is not likely that we will be able to establish that a rocket strike caused the explosion on the Boeing 747 because we just don't have enough parts of the plane intact. How the terrorists got there we don't yet know."

"Thank you, Colonel. I am sure we all appreciate your contribution."

"Major Viper, we would first like to say thank you for bringing several matters relating to the Heathrow incident to our attention. We appreciate you giving us your time to enable us to evaluate the information. Your knowledge and experience are invaluable. Major Viper, I can see from the map the location of the workshop and laboratory. It doesn't seem to be an obvious location to me. How did you find it?"

"I spent several hours observing this area. There was no real reason – just a gut feeling. I became aware that more persons were entering and leaving the building than I believed to be normal, especially during the dark hours. So I arranged an entry. Again we were lucky. As we entered one of the targets was just coming up through a trapdoor in the floor. Had we been later, I believe the trapdoor would have been concealed. We found no others there at that time, and I assume the one we caught was the caretaker. We took photographs and removed items for examination."

"Major Viper, according to Colonel Sheppard you said the terrorists wouldn't know you had found the workshop and removed some items. How can you be sure of that?"

"Well, sir, we can't be 100 per cent sure, but we did leave everything almost as we found it. The caretaker we killed, but we made it look as though he was drunk and fell down the entrance steps, hitting his head. We left no marks that might betray our presence."

"I see. Major Viper, can you explain your theory on the contamination of the water system? Is that a knowledge- or experience-based theory?"

"Sir, a lot of the theories and ideas I have put forward are based on my own ideas of the way things might have been done. In Afghanistan I observed the water system and noticed how the locals make use of it and how it becomes contaminated. They have no method of filtration other than by boiling, and often the water flowing into a village has been contaminated upstream. Sometimes a complete village goes down with cholera or something similar. I recalled that zinc entered the water supply in Camelford, Cornwall, and it entered after the water had passed through the filtration plant. I can see just how easily that could happen again, because no one is looking out for that to happen. The zinc spread through the water system and caused health problems. I believe the water could easily be contaminated deliberately. It is a possibility that has not been addressed because it has not yet happened, but it would be a major problem if it happened, and then we could be sitting in another meeting like this one."

"Major, you seem to believe that the terrorists' strategies will move away from using high explosives and towards biological and chemical warfare. Can you elaborate?"

"Sir, you can put it down to money. It costs money to buy explosives, and they have become more difficult to obtain. The bombs they use these days are often home-made using cheap, easily available materials. They have become larger and easier for us to locate, so the terrorists are having to look for more efficient weapons. And of course in the West we have the media, who broadcast details of all the best ways for terrorists to inflict the most damage they can on the Western world. Now, if I were Joe Terrorist, sitting in my cave and reading the Western papers, I would be reading every day about many different types of viruses and bacterial diseases, from the common cold to MRSA, etc., etc. So instead of buying expensive explosives and having the problem of delivering an explosive device to the target area I could use viruses to create mass destruction. I read in the paper that in the UK the sale of bottled water has gone through the roof, and the paper gives me details of where the water comes from and that the bottling plants are very simple and usually isolated; so it would be very easy to contaminate literally millions of bottles, which would be distributed all over the UK and Europe. I notice, gentlemen, that you are now looking with suspicion at the bottles of water on the desk in front of you. In this room are six bottles. If they had been contaminated, we would not know until later, when we all collapsed. Another method involves people. The papers reported that a group of persons returned from holiday and were struck down with a contagious virus. Then more persons were struck down and hospitals were closed etc., etc. Now, persons on holiday are a very easy target for contamination, and an easy way of spreading a contagious virus. So where can I obtain these viruses? Some I could manufacture myself. Alternatively I could employ persons with degrees in medical chemistry to find a new virus. But perhaps the best, cheapest and most readily available virus – and one which is highly contagious and not easy to detect – is the HIV virus. From the papers and television, we know that HIV is rife in Africa, and that it can be transmitted via bodily fluids, so that means we probably have millions of gallons of the virus literally walking around in Africa and other countries. It can be obtained freely and easily bottled or canned and transported anywhere in the world. Airport scanners would not detect the virus in a bottle of water or can of fluid. Yes, sir, I can see you are looking very hard at that bottle in front of you. At present we are reading about money laundering and basically honest people being used as mules to carry out illegal transactions, so people could be used as mules to carry virus packages into any country concealed in bottles of wine, packets of cigarettes, watches or cameras. Recently customs and excise found a vodka bottling plant in the back of a lorry, complete with a container containing gallons of possibly fake vodka. That could just as easily have been a virus-bottling plant. Customs and excise found it by accident, and they found it had been transported from Eastern Europe, so how did it end up in a warehouse in the UK without being spotted earlier? I hope these facts frighten you in the same way as they frighten me. Fake drink, drugs and tobacco are found every day in your local supermarkets, so you can imagine just how easy it would be to distribute virus-packed goods within the UK. Think how easy it is to advertise and distribute an item on the Internet. It would be very simple to distribute a Viagra pill contaminated with a deadly virus, for example. A long time ago I came to the conclusion that the time will come when the terrorist we have spent so much money and so many lives defending ourselves against will be able to sit at home in front of the fire while his mules cause havoc and suffering all over the world."

"Major I would like to hear about terrorist detection. Your report was very clear about how they would look. Can you elaborate?"

"As I see it, the average person does not usually notice details. Anything out of the ordinary is likely to be overlooked. For example, if you see a person wearing a uniform, you will probably notice he is a policeman, a ticket inspector or a bus or train driver; but if you were asked to describe the person's features, you could not. If the person was carrying a weapon, you would focus on that item. At airports we have scanners to detect weapons, but persons who look like terrorists are much more likely to be stopped and searched than those who don't look like terrorists. The person is from Asia: possible terrorist: stop. The person is from Europe: be careful, you might be challenged as a racist: let through. And so on. Sir, I believe that while we are killing persons in Afghanistan, who, let's face it, are really just defending their country from invaders and are no more a threat to our country than the price of fuel, the real terrorists are not hiding behind rocks in Asia; they are here, living next door or down the road. We now have over a million immigrants and they don't look English. They have come from all over the world. I say, put them in a line and ask the country's defenders, the security services, to pick out from the million ten who are real terrorists. Sir, I strongly believe that we have many cells of moles in this country. They are living normal, everyday lives. They might be workers in hospitals, doctors, workers in the emergency services or students in universities. They are all just waiting for the call. Oh, right – you detect and jail the person who hates the world and all the people in it and wants to die to make history – have his name in blood – but think for a minute. How did you detect that person? How? Well, he revealed himself. He travelled to Asia to a training camp; he made friends of a similar ideology; he went round buying bags of fertiliser; he was on websites illustrating terroristic ways. Do you really believe a real terrorist would reveal himself? During the post-mortem on the terrorist we killed at Heathrow he was found to be wearing blue contact lenses. This suggests that he realised his normal brown eyes would be a giveaway; the blue eyes enabled him to blend in. They gave him a Western appearance, just as my brown eyes allow me to blend in with the locals when I am in the East. They were clean-shaven with short hair, so they looked like normal Western-type citizens and did not attract any attention. The television pictures we have of the terrorist spokesman give the impression that he has spent some time in this country, and he too had blue eyes. He also seemed to be familiar with the layout and routine at Buckingham Palace. Had he already visited? Had he been shown round the palace as a tourist? Would anybody have noticed he was more interested in the layout than the priceless objects? Who knows – we might be looking for him in the wrong direction!"

"Well, Major, from what you say there doesn't seem to be much hope of defending our country. If what you have said is right, then our present methods are not good enough. Part of what you say might happen has already taken place. We need to up our game plan by many levels, and we must never sit back complacently and think we have reached the optimum level. Major, if these cells are being put in place, how do you think they will be communicated with? How do you think they can avoid our detection methods? How would you operate the network to keep it secure from detection?

"Sir, that's a very good question. To make sure the plot was not discovered, I would make sure that each cell was completely independent of the others. If they had no knowledge of one another, if one cell was compromised it would not matter."

"Major, that is all very well, but how would a cell communicate with other cells?"

"Sir, the communication method I would use would be a simple one. At present in most countries there is a common denominator that provides a method to communicate with anyone in Asia. It is a copy of an American idea: Bollywood. Virtually every minute of every day a Bollywood film is being produced. It is then distributed worldwide and is watched by almost all Asian persons. I would have my messages and instructions concealed in the credits, which are shown at the end of the film. I would use different dialects and a different code for each individual. How many persons watch the credits? How many persons could actually read and understand them? How many different dialects are there? How many Western persons can understand them? Even the prison service shows these films to keep the convicted persons happy. There is no censorship. They do not understand the film or its dialogue. Even convicted terrorists sitting in our prisons could receive information and instructions from home by this method. Our method of secretly recording conversations with visitors would be a waste of time and could be used against us. The American method of total isolation might seem inhumane, but it might be the best way. If we were to ban all films in prisons, we would have the European courts chasing us or riots happening.

"Another simple method of communication that could be used by sleepers in the UK is homing pigeons. Every year many thousands of homing pigeons are released in locations in Europe, and they fly undetected into Britain. This system was used in previous wars and proved very effective for transmitting information, and there is no reason why it can't be used again. It may already be in operation by terrorists worldwide.

"Also we should think about eggs – chickens' eggs. Thousands of eggs are imported into the UK from overseas. These are not scanned at airports. Coded messages could be printed on the outside or inserted inside the shell. Then the eggs could be transported to the required destination. Let's not forget that every city in the UK has shops, supermarkets, restaurants and takeaways all owned and run by possible sleepers; and they have regular deliveries of products, some of which come from their own countries. Are they checked? I very much doubt it.

"Another way to set up an operational cell would be through

the medical system. Many of the doctors in Britain are from Asia, and some of them could be high-ranking terrorists. Other terrorists could visit them without exciting suspicion. It would seem like a normal, everyday occurrence, but information could be being passed both ways between doctor and patient. These meetings would take place during normal surgery hours, and this could be happening in all the large cities in the UK. We have already had instances of malpractice by some of these overseas doctors – not just GPs, but hospital doctors as well. We need a whole lot more security personnel trawling the country and examining every aspect of everyday life."

"Major, you described infiltration by container ships as a problem. Can you expand on that?"

"Yes, sir. This island of ours has become the biggest cargo-dumping ground in the world. Every second we have cargo arriving from all over the world. Yes, I know we export some, but not anywhere near as much as we import. Now the imports come from everywhere, and our detection rate for drugs and counterfeit items is poor. If it is fifty per cent, we normally feel good. If customs and excise spot a few fake designer clothes, watches, tobacco or drugs, that makes the headlines and the British people think we are beating crime, but we are now facing terrorists who are expanding their global activities because it is becoming easier. If they can carry out a few more atrocities like the one at Heathrow, then the Western world will need to spend more of their resources on protecting their own countries. For instance, we have deployed 10,000 troops in Afghanistan and we have lost 500 men. We have killed thousands, which we say is a gain against terrorism, but we have now lost 50,000 at home. Look at the figures. You can hardly say we are winning. At this rate they will wipe us out before we wipe them out. In one act of terrorism they have destroyed more of the world's population than we or the Americans have achieved in the last decade. Going back to my answer to your earlier question, it will be a lot simpler for terrorists to import biological and chemical weapons into the UK than bombs and rockets. Not only are they very difficult to detect, but they are easy to deploy and able to destroy more persons and infrastructure at very little cost. Five gallons of a disease culture of some sort could be smuggled into the country in a five-gallon drum among 10 million others. The latest container ship has just docked at Southampton with 16,000 full containers on board. Could you detect that one five-gallon drum if it was in one of those 16,000 containers? The container city at Southampton has become so large that it receives some 2 million-plus containers each year, and also has thousands of employees. It would be quite easy to infiltrate such a large workforce in the same way as the terrorists have infiltrated the security system in Afghanistan. Every port is like another open gate into this country. I know the port security might be good, but good at what exactly? Good at detecting normal, everyday problems, but what about the once-in-a-lifetime abnormal problem? Gentlemen, our present capability of defending this country is minimal. The other day I paid a visit to a large home-improvement store. I could not count how many tins of paint were on display, and other containers, packets and tubes, all of which could be used to transport a more sinister material. Not many, if any, were made in this country. The items from outside the UK are counted in millions – probably billions. We had an advance warning when a bomb was discovered in the toner cartridge for a laser printer at Stansted Airport. That was being delivered by the UPS system and – guess what? – a UPS van was located at the palace. Coincidence? How many 'coincidences' do we need? I hope you have studied the UPS system of worldwide delivery, as I am sure the terrorists have. UPS use their own aeroplanes and airports, and probably their own security. Gentlemen, alarm bells should be ringing. Do you know how many batteries are imported? Do you know how many batteries are tested to make sure they are not loaded with something nasty? Not one. Well, gentlemen, our complacency has just had a whacking big dent banged into it by what has happened at Heathrow. Had we not detected the two chemical weapons installed in London and the one at Heathrow we would now be looking at 50,000 dead plus 6 million slowly dying. We would have 2 million unburied bodies, and the six persons in this room could be on the shortlist for burial. Gentlemen, I remember how stupid it seemed when I found out that zebra crossings were not installed by the council until the spot had a certain number of fatalities. What is the sense of that? We shouldn't have to wait till so many persons die before we put up a crossing. Do we have to wait until we have five atrocities like the one at Heathrow before we decide to do something to prevent them?"

"Major, do you yourself have a solution?"

"Sir, if we had 60 million completely British persons in the UK, we would still lose. At present we have a million immigrants from many different countries. They can't all be terrorists. But atrocities aren't just carried out by terrorists. It could be someone who wants to make a name, or money, for himself. Just think: out of that million, if just ten were killers, could we detect them? At the moment our best chance is if they give themselves away. We were not aware that the terrorists were in the palace until they told us so, and at that time we did not know they were also at Heathrow. Again, we found out by chance. Had we not discovered them, they could have melted away and we might have assumed Heathrow was just an unfortunate accident. And if, in the area around Heathrow, persons were poisoned, we might have put that down to the leakage of chemicals from the scene of the accident. At present we are changing the way we attack other countries, with the introduction of drone warfare. We are designing and manufacturing remote-controlled flying bombs which can be sent to all parts of the world to destroy persons who may or may not be a threat. We should think of the potential consequences. We should take into account the scenes of carnage at New York (9/11) and Heathrow. How were these two events and others like them able to happen? Quite simply because we had manufactured the hardware to make them possible! We should be concerned that manufacturing the weapons for drone warfare could result in these weapons being used against the very countries that produced the weapons in the first place!"

"Colonel, can you add any more to the findings of Major Viper?"

"Sirs, did we sit back after the bombing of the London Tube system thinking that wasn't too bad? What did we actually learn from that? Did we assume that was as bad as it could get? You know, it was hardly a major terrorist strike, and yet we did not prevent it happening. We just cleaned up after the event, and hoped. Yes, gentlemen, we just hoped it wouldn't happen again. I expect you ordered more resources, more monitoring of emails, phone calls, etc., etc., but that method goes back to looking-for-the-bad-apples-in-a-barrel syndrome. Now we have a situation in which 50,000 died and Heathrow was totally wiped out. It makes all other terrorist attacks seem like a walk in the park by comparison."

"Gentlemen, what happens next? Let's say the incident at Heathrow was caused by twenty-five terrorists and there are 60 million persons in UK – a million are immigrants and only twenty-five are terrorists. But suppose we open our borders for another 30 million immigrants with the same proportion of terrorists. We would then have 775 terrorists in a population of 90 million. Could we one day reach a point where the immigrants take over the country by majority rule, and not by bombing and killing? Could the next Bin Laden or Saddam Hussein be the Prime Minister of the UK. We have already surrendered control of our own country by agreeing with the demands from Brussels. If the non-British persons form a majority in this country, then I expect Brussels will give them control of the country as well?"

"Thank you, Major. I believe I am speaking for all of us when I say thank you for your advice, your honest opinions and your amazing contributions to our meeting."

"Colonel, do you have you any more to say before we terminate our meeting?"

"Sirs, my final words relate to everything that has been said today. I hope that all the points brought up will be taken into account and some good will come of this meeting. We have had not just warnings, but actual events to learn from. We should also take into account the mess-up of the security arrangements at the Olympics. The army had to be brought in to cover that. We have seen that the security provided by the private sector is of little use to combat a major terrorist attack. It is no good having bomb disposal squads if they are not there when required. We should have plans in place for the urgent deployment of trained army personnel at places like airports, container ports and nuclear power stations. All points of entry to our island should be secure – totally secure. No, sirs, having armed policemen walking about is not a secure method of defence. Before they could challenge a real terrorist they would be dead and their weapons taken and used against the public.

"We should also seriously consider a new independent army unit capable of rapid response and deployment to take control of any situation involving hostages, explosives or biological attack. In other words, we need another SAS unit permanently based and operational in the UK, and only the UK. We must learn from what has happened at Heathrow that because we had deployed most of our SAS regiment overseas we had left our back door wide open. Our cities were not fully protected. Also we need another rapid-response unit to be fully trained to provide medical help in the event of chemical or biological attack anywhere in the UK. This unit could be deployed to assist and advise local hospitals. It is no good having the best hospitals in the world if the situation confronting them is beyond their capabilities. We should be aware that admitting a contaminated person into one of our hospitals could result in the deaths of everyone in the hospital, and everyone in the city where the hospital is located. If we need to have a police state for our own security and safety, then let's have a proper one and not the type we have at present. Let's properly protect our island from air, land and sea. Let's use simple common sense instead of ignorance. Let's replace the political word 'quantity' with 'quality'. If we can't do these things, then we might as well just hand over the entire country to whoever wants it. At least then more of the present population might remain alive and well."

"Well, Viper, what are your thoughts after our meeting?"

"Sheppard, I must admit that, no matter how many times we have these meetings, afterwards I still think and feel the same.

I would be very surprised if my beliefs were any different!"

"Viper, why do you think that is so? You must have hope. It might be lodged somewhere deep inside your brain."

"Sheppard, if only I knew that was true! When you look at what is on the opposite side of the table, you know you are debriefing to persons who really don't have a clue. They don't seem to be able to understand what I was saying! They have never been out in the field. They sit there listening carefully, making notes, asking questions, but I know and you know that I can't rely on them. They don't have the physical capabilities necessary for defending the country. All they can actually do is to have even more meetings and pass on the details. At the end of the day we just have even more details, even more knowledge, but we don't have any more experience until a crisis occurs. Let's just call it an event! An event happens; then what happens? We have more meetings to see if we can stop the same event happening again, but it is unlikely that the very same event will ever happen again! What is depressing is that common sense tells me that if we had the correct persons at the top the event could have been avoided in the first place! You know, Sheppard, back in the proper world, when you left school and started your first job you had to start at the bottom and work your way up to the top. That meant that persons had to have knowledge and experience before they became foremen, sergeants, captains. That was truly a common-sense approach. OK, you had persons who became leaders by wealth, but there was a backbone of persons who were qualified by experience and ability. Now we have leaders whose only experience is three years on a university campus, but they do have a degree!"

"Viper, I am right behind you every step of the way in your thinking. At the meeting today I tried to imagine how they would cope if they were out in the field. They would not have a clue how to identify or tackle a real live terrorist situation. They would not even be able to kill to defend themselves. They would lose their own lives as well as endangering the lives of others. For all they knew we two might have been terrorists plotting to kill them, but they would never have known!"

"You say that, Sheppard, but I wouldn't be surprised if they have very suspicious minds! I could see suspicion in their faces as the meeting went on, and it would not surprise me one little bit if we were put under surveillance and have our details and records looked at and our phones tapped, etc., etc."

"Viper, I won't laugh. Because I know you so very well, I know you are not joking."

"Sheppard, I spend many moments thinking about the world, and particularly about our country. And I try to understand why if common sense is claimed by so many, do so few actually use it? In the papers I once read that a teenage boy was put into jail. His crime was that he broke into many new cars, all of different manufacture, and the manufacturers were so upset that they wanted the maximum sentence given to him to teach him a lesson. Now, where is the common sense? Jail is the capital of the world in educating persons to have a criminal mind; he would be sure to pass on his expert knowledge to others. Common sense tells me, yes, give him a quick shock – show him what it can be like in jail – but then the manufacturers should club together and give him a job to help design security locks. After all, the persons they were already employing to design locks were not doing a very good job if a teenager could bypass their security so easily. The same should apply to tackling the global terrorist problem. We have the same lack of common sense from the Americans. Just count how many bombs your terrorist has set off and add up the damage. Now count how many bombs the Americans have dropped and add up the damage. Take a long, hard look at the cost of each side's effort. What about the fact that the terrorist uses the very hardware that the Western world provides. The terrorist doesn't need to be an Einstein; he just assembles the material we manufacture. Not only that, but we provide all the know-how on the Internet! And – you know what? – Joe Terrorist doesn't even have to sit and think. The media does that for him, and even supplies him with information in his language so he doesn't need to translate! What about drones? OK, the Americans are proving they can be deployed successfully! But what is to stop the terrorists obtaining drones and using them against us? We know from experience that weapon hardware is available where money is available! What about that single disgruntled person! The drone maker who decides to put himself in the history books! Just think of the acclaim he could achieve if he used a drone to kill the President sitting at his desk in the White House or our own Prime Minister walking his dog in the grounds of Number 10. What about the media giving out the location for the next meeting of Western leaders attending the next European summit or the next G8 summit! That would be a very tasty target for the terrorist to destroy! Would the ring of steel – the security lockdown – be able to prevent a drone attack? I don't think so. I know the Americans would soon be there to tell us who was to blame and who to bomb, but, as usual, it would be after the event! Sheppard, on my last visit to the States I visited the retired aeroplane boneyards in Arizona, California and New Mexico. These are amazing places, probably the size of London, and each has thousands and thousands of old and not so old planes from the small to the large and the very large, from the very fast to the very slow, just lines and lines of them as far as your eye can see. It was quite a moving and eerie experience to stand and see them. But a few terrorists with a basic knowledge of the workings of a plane and technical ability could work on some of the planes without being detected, and they could soon have some of the planes up and ready to fly. Not only that, but they could take off and attack any of the cities close by and even those within a couple of hundred miles or so. I am sure they could be made airworthy quite quickly, and by the time the Americans had fighter planes up to intercept and destroy them the terrorists could have carried out their attacks. I think the Americans need to have a very close look at some of their stockpiles of weapons. They might not be weapons of mass destruction, but they would be hugely destructive in the wrong hands. The materials are readily available to build drones as well as conventional planes."

"Viper, those are my thoughts exactly. The persons at the

top can have no real idea about how much of a threat these goatherds and farmers are to world stability, and it's all of our own making. The blighters use our weapons and throw our knowledge of warfare straight back into our own faces, and they cause far more mayhem than we ever anticipated. When you brought up the subject of contaminating the UK water supply, the SS (as we call them) seemed a bit concerned about how much you knew; yet a tabloid paper recently ran an article on that very subject. The government were concerned about a possible terrorist attack on the UK's water supply, but they reassured the public that there was no real danger. They said they had installed adequate security. When I read that I thought, 'What a stupid thing to say!' I mean, if the terrorists had not already considered attacking the water supply, after reading that they probably would. And what about all the nutcases we already have in the country? Because the government have said there's no risk, they would love to prove them wrong! Your ideas refer to a simple attack on the pipelines, not the pumping stations or reservoirs!"

"Yes, Sheppard, I read the article and thought the same. Again common sense was not applied! Ever since I was in primary school I have known that if you tell somebody it's wet paint, don't touch, they probably will. I would have thought by now someone in the government would realise that there is no security system in the wide world which cannot be breached. They are designed by men with specialist knowledge, but there are always equally knowledgeable men who can get round them. We know from the number of cyberattacks on the Internet how easy it is to penetrate a computer network and download data. That is how the spying departments obtain a lot of their information. The very data we use to defend ourselves could also be used against us. The next number-one superpower will be China. The Chinese have complete departments in the military and elsewhere staffed by persons who have the ability to infiltrate every computer network in the world! They probably already know all my own details, my family details, and where I had my last meal and my last holiday, and they may have pirated that information from some American spying system! The Chinese don't need to squander a vast sum of money setting up a worldwide surveillance network; they just log into the systems of America and other countries. When governments say they have installed adequate security, the terrorists probably fall about laughing! As everybody knows, the reservoirs, pumping stations and million miles of piping have very few personnel to observe, identify and report any breaches of security. It would be impossible to install and monitor enough CCTV cameras to protect the infrastructure! The very simple methods I spoke about could be used with devastating impact! I just hope that no terrorist is thinking on the same line.

"I believe the terrorist of the future will come from within and not from outside! The way the world is progressing we might not have to be so concerned about being infiltrated by the robed, bearded ones, but by high-flying rockets carrying weapons of mass destruction. Again we have to thank the Americans and ourselves for showing the world what a nuclear explosion can achieve! You might say our airspace has been opened and our air security has been breached. Let's not forget our noble protector the sea. Our island security has also been breached by the Channel Tunnel. As well as that, someone has suggested that you could park tankers and container ships in the Channel from Dover to Calais and walk across from France into Britain!"

"And, Viper, I believe the Chinese have every intention of taking over the world eventually to feed all their own people! Let's face it, no one will be bigger or more powerful than them; they already have an invisible army located in every single country of the world! America is a typical example. You can see, when you visit their Chinatown, that they have their very own way of living, their own policing, religion and laws. The Chinese have built several tanker-type submarines which they say are for cargo transport. Ah, they don't need to tell us. We know they could also be used to transport a complete army and equipment to virtually anywhere in the world. They can do that without being detected, as the Americans found out when a Chinese nuclear-armed submarine popped up next to their aircraft carrier in the Gulf without being detected by the worldwide surveillance centre in Washington, the Pentagon. I believe the Chinese while on the surface did flash a message asking the captain of the aircraft carrier, 'Did you order a takeaway?' before they disappeared again. Typically, the Pentagon's first reaction was that their aircraft carrier personnel were all drunk and it was all a joke; but then the captain relayed a picture of the submarine and the Pentagon personnel all wet themselves. It goes to show that you can't always depend on the Americans. When I watch nature programmes showing how ants behave and cooperate in a colony it makes me wonder if there are a billion Chinese watching and learning. The way they have migrated from China to settle in every single corner of the world is very ant-like. It might not be in my lifetime, but I believe that one day the Chinese will control the world, and other nations will be their servants, dancing to their tune. There will be small pockets of resistance and persons will fight to regain their independence. It's a pity we can't all live together and work for each other and enjoy what is just a short time in the world instead of all the time and money being spent on spreading death and destruction. That goes on every single minute of every single day just so one person can be top dog! It's really all about wealth and power – two goals that persons spend their whole lives trying to achieve. How very futile the whole idea is! In the end you can never take it with you into the next world, so really what is the point?"

CHAPTER ELEVEN

A meeting of ministers was called at 10 Downing Street.

"Welcome, everybody. On the table in front of you is a copy of the transcript of an interview with a woman called Hanna Thomas, whose life was changed by the disaster at Heathrow. When I came across it I found it very moving. It highlights facts which at first seemed to be beyond the realms of fancy. The interview moved me so much that I wanted to share it with you all. When you are out and about, meeting your constituents, bear this in mind. It may help you to understand the trauma suffered by those thousands directly or indirectly involved with the disaster we now label as Heathrow Ground Zero. Without a doubt this atrocity was one of the darkest pages in the world's history. I trust that this and future generations will learn from what has happened."

TRANSCRIPT

Today we are privilege – no, deeply honoured – to be able to talk to a very special lady who can remember reading the very first paper this paper published many years ago.

"Welcome, Hanna Thomas. Are you all right, my love? I can understand this must be another very traumatic moment in your life and if you feel distressed at any time or wish to stop, please just say. Hanna, can I asked your age?"

"Yes, sir. I am sixty-two years old, and still in control of most of myself. I do have constant flashbacks and keep repeating myself, but I will try to the best of my ability to be helpful."

"Hanna, could you now tell us about the dramatic change to your life recently?"

"Yes, sir. A few days, weeks ago I had a normal life and a complete family – not just a family, but a complete family of some twelve very wonderful people. Now, sir, I have nobody – not a single person. I have lost the whole lot – my life. I have lost my world. That world disappeared in a puff of smoke, just like that. I had no warning. I had no time – no time to say goodbyes. Everything – everybody I knew just vanished in smoke and fire and into thin air."

"Hanna, I cannot imagine for one second the pain and grief you must be feeling. You must be the bravest person I have met in my lifetime. We all must be eternally grateful that you are able to share your grief and suffering with us so that we might better understand how others suffering from grief might be feeling. Hanna, could you tell us more about your wonderful family and the life you all had together?"

"Well, sir, my old man – my husband, Thomas – we had been together since we left school. I can remember him sharpening my pencils for me, and carrying my satchel to and from the school gate every day. And the notes and cards he made himself – he posted them through my letter box when I was stuck indoors because of the chickenpox and measles. We all seemed to end up with them in them days. Tom was a very able worker and had a good job, so we were able to marry and set up a good home and look after and feed our three children. We had two boys, John and Peter, and our daughter, Susan. John was married to Jean. They were blessed with two lovely children, Kevin and Mary. Kevin wanted to be a policeman and had applied for a job at the airport. Peter and his wife, Margaret, had two boys, Ben and Tim. Our daughter, Susan, married Jim. She was much younger than my boys – a sort of a late arrival. Well, we had not expected to have any more after the boys were born; so Susan was a surprise, but a very nice one. I am not sure how our Susan happened. Anyway, we were the oldest mum and dad at primary school, and Susan took some stick as the other kids thought we were her grandparents – not that we minded. She was a good daughter. Sorry, sir."

"All right, Hanna, take your time. Rest if you want to."

"Thank you, sir. Well, Susan was expecting our first grandchild – a very exciting event for Tom and me. We had cancelled our holiday so we would be close when the baby was born. We hoped the others might get move on so we could have a few more – the more the merrier is what I say. Susan only had a few more days to work before she started her maternity leave, so I was looking forward to spending some time with her and shopping for the baby. Tom and I were going to buy the pram – well, more the latest modern-type pushchair. They don't seem to go for the old-fashioned prams like we used to use; they're more space-age and fold-up these days. We had decided with Susan and Jim we would wait until the baby was born. I must say I was hoping she would have twins so we could buy a posh double-buggy type."

"Are you OK, Hanna? Would you like to stop and rest for a while?"

"No, I am all right, sir. Just a memory flashing by took me away briefly. I am all right."

"Hanna, would you tell us about that day which changed everything for you?"

"Oh, yes, sir. It started out as just a normal day. All the family except myself and Tom worked at the airport in different departments – at the terminals and thereabout. The morning was all right – just a normal morning. About two thirty we had a call from Susan at work. She was not feeling well and asked if Tom could pick her up. Normally she would come home with Jim, but he was working at one of the other terminals and she couldn't get hold of him. So Tom came in from the greenhouse and got cleaned up and set off. I was watching TV. Time went on and there was no sign of Tom and Susan, so I imagined that they had stopped at shops or the doctor's; so I was not worried. About six o'clock the TV news said there had been a plane crash at the airport. Again I was not worried as my family did not work for the plane side of things – more in the offices and maintenance. Time went on and there was more news on the TV, but no word from any of my family so I assumed they must be all right. I tried to phone to see if Jean or Mary were home – I knew Jim worked late, so he would not be home yet. Then I tried Tom's mobile, but there was no answer; so I went and checked in the greenhouse, as Tom often left his jacket with the phone in there. But there was nothing. I now felt very alone and was starting to feel distressed. I looked at the TV. The news was showing some fires burning at the airport and reporting about traffic problems, which made me wonder if the family were caught up and stuck in traffic; so I tried contacting one of them with my mobile. Again there was no connection, but again that was not unusual as mobile-phone connection around the airport is notoriously bad at the best of times. It's something to do with all the electronics and radar contraptions. By the time midnight came I was very lonely, very lost. There was no information from anywhere or anybody. I checked with some neighbours and friends who worked at the airport, but nothing was known by anybody – not a single bloody thing. The TV news was not very helpful – just flames and people talking what to me was gibberish. Nothing seemed honest or believable. It was just like some disaster movie. I was expecting any moment that my lot would arrive home happy and laughing as usual, and wanting a nice cuppa.

"You know, sir, even days later I was not any the wiser about what actually happened to my family. It was not possible for me to accept, believe, that they would never come home – not all of them gone. Surely one or more of them would be alive! It wasn't possible to lose all of them in just a few hours – surely that could never happen! Surely the good Lord wouldn't let that happen – not to good, loving people! Surely not.

"Yes, sir, the pain I felt, when the truth jumped up and gripped, ripped my heart completely out. The pain is still there and will be for evermore. I was strangled by emotional grief. It engulfed me. My eyes become red and sore, but no tears can flow any more. My body has been completely drained dry. I am completely dried up. There is not a single teardrop anywhere. I know my face looks so gaunt, but sometimes I feel totally emptied of emotions. I am unable to enjoy a smile or even a slight grimace with pain. There is just a vacant wilderness of grief and total disbelief. I am told that only the living can pray, but there seems to be no point in saying a prayer. What is the point? How could I offer a prayer? What would I say? I've just lost everything I ever had. I can't wake up in the morning and feel happy and look forward to the day in front of me; instead I wake up and dread the emptiness, dread the time in front of me. I feel so dried up. I sit and look at twelve graves. My memories will always be with me, but they can never replace the family I once had. These memories are so very precious to me, but they can't take away the pain and grief in my heart. I am unable to cry, unable to find consolation, unable to say goodbye.

"Yes, I would like to know exactly what happened to my family; yes, I would like to know that they suffered no pain; yes, I would like to know who was responsible; yes, I would like to know they have been punished for the harm they caused; yes, I can now understand the grief that so many others are feeling. But no, no, I don't want to link arms with all the other grieving people who have survived this holocaust. Who should I blame – the bad men of the world or the mothers who gave birth to them in the first place? Perhaps they were brought up wrongly. Why, oh why did they need to kill? Why did they need to take my family from this earth? What exactly was the bloody purpose of all this? What exactly is the bloody purpose of wars? What is the bloody purpose of living and killing? Who can tell me the actual purpose, the actual reason? Please, God Almighty, please tell me before I go insane. . . ."

EPILOGUE

Persons should be frightened by what could happen in the world we live in. Take a few minutes to look at the history books, and look carefully at the historic events that occur in your own lifetime. You will realise that nothing has changed. The world we live in is in fact little different from how it was thousands of years ago, though we have often been told we will have a better world in the future. Does it really matter if we have more money and are able to travel around the world and see more places? Will that mean a better life for us? Is it so important to have a better life that you will tread on people to achieve that? You should expect others to want the very same as you do, and they might use your methods to achieve it.

If a government decides that another country doesn't meet its requirements, that country is attacked and many people die in the attempt to bring that country and its people into line with those requirements. The people of the invaded country are expected to fall into line, but they will borrow the technology and weapons that have been used against them to enable them to retaliate at a later date.

The world of today may seem different from that of biblical times, but the people behave in a similar way. One difference is that we now see the happenings on our TV screens and even watch the happenings in real time. In biblical times a disaster in one part of the world could happen and the only persons who knew about it might be the persons in the vicinity. Before ships were able to travel long distances persons did not get involved in other countries. And – you know what? – they didn't want to. They could have a good happy life as they were. Without a doubt the world's troubles started when larger boats were built. The bigger the boats, the further they could travel and the more persons could travel in them, and the more counties they could plunder, take over and bully. When persons enter the UK and steal and plunder we are outraged and lock them up in prisons, but in fact all they are doing is copying what we carried out many years ago. We sent persons out to kill and to plunder, and we said that was the right thing to do. And just to prove we were right we knighted and honoured the persons and wrote admiringly about their exploits, and produced history books to celebrate all the 'good' deeds and brave exploits, and swept the bad things out of sight. It is very difficult to explain to persons we call terrorists that what they are doing is wrong when we have done the same in the past.

What is happening in the world is the same that happens every day in the school playground. If one child has a bag of sweets, the other children want some as well; others will want to take them for themselves by fighting, bullying and stealing. In some countries people are short of water and food; they have no PlayStation, no electricity, no gas. That was not such a problem until they learnt that others had all these things; and they learn from history books that the wealthier nations got these things by waging war around the world, plundering and killing. They reason that they can have the same by doing the same. Perhaps instead of using brutal force and waging war every person of every country in the world should have exactly the same standard of living. Then there would be no need for global terrorism and no need for countries to perform violent acts of questionable legality against one another.